THE CURIOUS WORLD OF
SHELLEY VENDOR

To Rhiannon
Enjoy the adventure!

THE CURIOUS WORLD OF
SHELLEY VENDOR

by
Colin R. Parsons

Cover Illustration by Derek Jones

The Curious World of Shelley Vendor

Copyright © Colin R Parsons 2009

ISBN 978-0-9570278-1-7

Published

by

TallyBerry

United Kingdom

Printed by Glenside Printing

Acknowledgements

Special thanks to:

My wife Jan for all the dedication and loyalty she has shown over the years, from the very beginning. Without her pushing me onwards, none of my journey would have been possible. Kristoffer and Ryan, my two sons, for all their support. Mam, who always believed in me and is always there with a helping hand. I love you, Mam.

Elsie, no longer with us, but believed in everything I did. Derek Jones, a very dear and close friend; he also illustrated the cover of this book and helped me on many of my other projects. His artwork is always wonderfully orchestrated and captivating. Lynne Francis, my wife's best friend and the person who did the first editorial refinements to the Shelley Vendor story.

A special thank you to *you* for reading and enjoying my books

Prologue

Shelley was adopted by Mr and Mrs Vendor when she was a baby. She is now thirteen, and being a teenager brings many problems. To add to that, she's also accident-prone. Combine those two elements with the fact that she also likes reading . . . oops! – and you have an accident-prone teenager nerd. Well, that's how the Scrag Girls see it. They are the school bullies and look for trouble at every turn. Everyone fears them and Shelley often tries avoiding them if possible. They often cause problems for her or just make fun of her, which leaves her pretty much unhappy.

On the other hand, though, she has friendship in the shape of Katie Hinge. Katie is the same age as Shelley and also likes to read and do things teenagers do. But she's a little more cautious than her clumsy friend and mostly keeps herself to herself. She has helped Shelley out of many an unintentional scrape. They enjoy each other's company, in school and outside.

There's a school trip taking place on World Book Day, a trip to a venue where there's lots and lots of famous authors. Shelley and Katie's favourite author is at the show. They are very keen to see him and get their books signed. Also at this exciting exhibition is a rather unusual and very expensive book called, 'Secrets in Time'. It's the crowning glory of the whole event, but there are others who have a more sinister interest in the book. Strange things happen that only Shelley can see!

This is where Shelley Vendor's curiosity takes over and a thrilling adventure begins.

Chapter 1

World Book Day

Shelley was still sleepy after being wrenched from her dreams by her mother's ranting from downstairs. So sleepy, in fact, that as she wandered aimlessly across the landing; she just missed the slippers scattered loosely and dangerously in her path. She also skimmed precariously past the rollerblade, abandoned awkwardly on the corner of the stairs. She even managed to avoid the towel that hung partly over the banister; it lay coiled like a bear trap, waiting for its victim. Having avoided all the near misses, she unfortunately didn't step squarely onto the top step, slightly catching the tip of her heel on the edge. Her right foot slid off the first step, closely followed by her left and the rest of her body.

Whoosh! There was a cold rush of air and a jerk. Shelley descended relatively slowly at first, but with the gathering momentum of travel she sped up. Her bottom acted as half-brake and half-buffer connecting with each of the eighteen stairs. Thud...thud...thud...thud...thud! Her eyes flickered open and shut with each bounce. She tried to call out but couldn't. 'Ouch, ouch, ouch, ouch,' was all that echoed in her mind on her relentless journey to the passageway floor. Halfway down, and Shelley began to see double, and even triple, as her eyes bounced about in her head like balls in a lottery tombola. The seat of her pyjama bottoms heated up under the intense friction, and her backside began to steadily glow as red as a traffic light! She clenched her teeth and closed her eyes tight shut

1

and waited for the inevitable impact at the bottom. And then it came...

On the last step, like a pellet from a slingshot, she bounced off and sailed through the air... coming to land face-down on the passageway carpet, knocking all the wind out of her lungs. She lay still for a few moments trying to catch her breath, between spitting out fibres of carpet thread.

'Oooohh,' she groaned. Her eyes slowly focused, reflecting red from her glowing cheeks. Still panting heavily, she managed to right herself and sat up. Then took in one huge mouthful of air, let out a long-winded puff and vigorously shook her head from side to side. The ordeal was over, but in the life of Shelley Vendor, this was a day-to-day occurrence. Clumsiness was part of her existence.

'Are you all right, dear?' her mother called out with concern, on her way from the kitchen. Shelley was always 'all right', ironically. Even the most animated fall didn't injure her normally, just the odd bruise. This thirteen year old was made of tough stuff.

'Yes mum I'm fine,' she answered, and they both strolled into the kitchen for breakfast together. And then it dawned on her. 'Mum! It's World Book Day,' she said beaming with joy.

'Yes I know, dear. You've been talking about it for months.' Mrs Vendor gave a pleasant smile.

'I hope Niloc Snosrap is there, mum. His new book looks fab.' She looked at her mother, filled with a deep excitement.

'Niloc who?' Her mother tut-tutted. 'The names you come out with, Shell. Now never mind about who's where, eat your toast and drink your tea or you'll be late.' Mrs Vendor was already pulling out the ironing board and the iron, to fight off the 'clothes monster' that lay in wait in the corner of the room.

Shelley took the hint and quickly ate her breakfast, dressed, and off she went to school.

'Shelley Vendor... Shel-ley Vendor. Oh, do concentrate, girl!' Mrs Gillies called out abruptly, reading the names on the register. She was a rather tall, thin woman, with deep, beady eyes. She also had a long, pointed nose which seemed to pull and crease the skin on her face. She was also the 'deputy head' and took everything very seriously, to the point of pain. The whole class were standing in line in the school yard.

Shelley felt a sharp dig in her ribs and quickly blinked her eyes and turned a deep shade of red, dropping her rucksack in the process, to the howls of laughter from the other girls.

'Silence!' Mrs Gillies screeched and peered menacingly at each and every pupil.

'Uh, here Mrs Gillies,' Shelley gulped and answered her call. She took a deep breath and stooped down to retrieve her bag. Shelley was tall and thin and her clothes rarely fitted, hanging loosely, giving her a frumpy look. Shelley also wore spectacles at times, framing her pale long face, which in itself shouldn't have been a problem, but she felt a bit of a nerd wearing them. She quickly snatched her bag from the ground and peered over her specs when she stood back up. The usual comments followed: 'What a tool you are, Vendor,' which came from the crowd, and 'Can't you do anything right?' The hurtful comments came mainly from the bullying Scrag Girls.

'Q-u-i-e-t, I won't tell you again!' Mrs Gillie's tones sailed through the air like a machine gun on overload. Katie stood at Shelley's side and shrugged her shoulders in sympathy.

'Never mind, Shell, come on,' she said gently patting her shoulder. Katie was Shelley's best friend since she'd moved to Timpton, deep in the heart of England. No one else would give her the time of day, but Katie Hinge befriended her, and they were inseparable. They shared the same love of books and many other interests.

All were gathered by the coach area at Timpton Comprehensive School, waiting patiently and very excited at the thought of missing lessons for the day. They were all going to an exhibition celebrating 'World Book Day.' Shelley had been excited about going for months, and so too was Katie. It was a frosty March morning and the air was heavy on the lungs. They stamped their feet and briskly rubbed their hands, waiting for the school bus to arrive.

Suddenly, the sound of a roaring engine echoed from the nearby housing estate and, sure enough, the grey-painted old bus chugged its way to the entrance. It came to a stop outside the open gates and its engine rattled and gave a whoosh as it settled.

'Stay where you are until I say you can go,' Mrs Gillies commanded. She then turned in the direction of the bus and made her way to the driver. The children momentarily were left in the charge of Miss Shanks. Miss Shanks feared the formidable Mrs Gillies with good reason. 'Shanksy', as the girls called her, was a very nice person, but she was often shouted down in front of the children by the deputy head. Most of the pupils felt sorry for her, that is, except for the Scrag Girls, who felt sympathy for no one. Nobody dared cross them, and everybody avoided them whenever possible.

Mr Jones, a robust figure, stepped off the platform of the coach and squared up to the deputy head to discuss the details of the journey. He often drove the school children on their many days out. He always tried to relieve the tense atmosphere inside the bus by putting on a CD of the children's favourite tunes whilst on the way back from a day out. Once they had finished their chinwag they parted company and she shuffled back to the eager children.

'Right, follow me to the bus and file on one at a time,' and she turned once more toward the bus. 'Don't dawdle, Miss Shanks, get a move on,' she said sharply. Soon everyone was pouring onto the coach. Poor Tina Sprockett unwisely sat on the back seat, forgetting the golden rule, and was soon ejected forcibly.

'Get off me,' she complained bitterly, as she delved inside her bag, but she soon cowered when Jade Pew, the leader of the Scrag Girls, shot her a piercing glare.

'Move, Sprockett, or I'll rocket you through the window,' the leader announced to the wails of laughter from the rest of the gang.

Sensibly the two friends Shelley and Katie sat at the front and immediately exploded into a chattering frenzy, though soon to be hushed by their less than happy teacher. Soon everyone was settled into the journey as the old bus chugged along the motorway.

It seemed to take an age, just sitting on the coach, but eventually, the bus took a right turn and there in front of them a big sign stood proud: "THIS WAY TO Tellington Arts World ". Chattering filled the whole of the coach until the raised, stern voice of Mrs Gillies shrieked over everyone else's.

'Q-u-i-e-t...' Everyone obeyed instinctively. Then the rickety old bus came to a trembling halt. The whooshing of air dominated, and the doors folded away. Under supervision of the overbearing deputy head, the pupils disembarked in an orderly fashion. As usual, the Scrag Girls pushed their way to the front, to the annoyance of all, but no one dared complain.

'Hurry along there,' Mrs Gillies puffed out her cheeks in annoyance. Shelley stepped off the platform and Katie followed. Katie gazed at the arts building and her mouth dropped open.

'This is amazing, Shell.' Katie gasped in awe. Tellington Arts World was a vast sight to behold. The building itself was a modern masterpiece. The whole structure was made of a million angles and long sloping inserts. The entrance was a giant glass affair with a triangular overhanging canopy that opened into a sweeping foyer. Every part of the outside of the building was made in mirrored glass. A massive banner hung over front with the words "Welcome to World Book Day" emblazoned upon it. There was quite a queue forming and Mrs Gillies swept passed the crowds and made her way to an official standing to one side. After a few moments she reappeared and called Miss Shanks.

'Right everyone. Follow Miss Shanks and I, come on quickly... Oh don't dawdle, Shelley Vendor, you're falling behind.' Her voice bore into Shelley's head like a hammer drill. She should have been used to it by now, but it still irritated her. Once inside, Katie and Shelley became very excited. Everything wondrous about the outside continued on the inside in the shape of perfection. The floor was reflective and shiny and the interior panelling of plastic and steel shone throughout. They were all stood in a line and were waiting patiently to go further inside. There was a counter inside the foyer with a cloakroom attendant standing the other side of it. Miss Shanks told the children to hand in their coats and keep hold of the ticket to retrieve them later. Shelley followed Katie and took off her coat as she walked. It was a short woollen jacket and Shelley accidentally stood on one of the sleeves that dangled on the floor. True to her clumsy form, her foot rested on it, causing it to act just like a sled on the shiny surface. She went skidding along the tiles, balancing on one leg and shot past Katie like a rocket. Katie looked on to see Shelley make it to the front of the queue before anyone else. It had happened so fast that no one else noticed except the attendant, who smiled warmly. Shelley was tempted to stay at the front, but after a short consideration she went back to her place in the queue alongside her friend.

'That was amazing, Shell,' Katie chuckled.

After depositing their coats, they stood waiting patiently together in the main queue to the event. There was a free-standing display of cards and bookmarks in triangular style settings placed on glass shelving next to them. One particular multicoloured bookmark caught Shelley's eye and curiously she took a closer look. Katie was otherwise occupied, staring at the many thousands of twinkling lights set in the ceiling like a scene from outer space. Something caught Katie's attention and she tilted her head just in time to see Shelley reach for the brightly coloured card.

'Shell, no!' she called and Shelley turned her attention to Katie and pulled away. But a sharp nudge from Vicky Temple knocked her arm forward. At first it seemed as though the delicate structure was unharmed. Then piece by piece the whole exhibit suddenly came crashing down! All eyes were now set firmly on Shelley and a smooth curved grin beamed from Vicky's mouth. From nowhere, what seemed like a million officials spewed out of the infrastructure and behind them, Mrs Gillies. Her eyes were fixed and her expression damning. She opened her mouth wide to express her utter disappointment when she was stopped in her prime...

'It wasn't her fault, Mrs Gillies...' There was a short silence and Miss Shanks stepped forward and continued, 'It was Vicky Temple. I saw her push Shelley.'

Without anymore ado Mrs Gillies' attention turned immediately to Vicky and a deep fear filled the mischievous girl's very soul.

'I-I didn't do it,' she protested with a pathetic streak of forged innocence, but Mrs Gillies was having none of it.

'Your parents will pay for all the damage here. I'll phone them later.'

One short, fat gentleman with an 'Arts World' tag clipped to the lapel of his uniform spoke to the deputy head.

'There's not really much damage, Mrs Gillies, but the children are going to have to take a little more care.'

He shot a steely glare at Vicky and she blew a deep long breath of gratitude. 'You can go through now,' he said. 'Once you get to the main hall, you can all have a free run inside.' He nodded to Mrs Gillies and turned toward some other group waiting for his attention.

'Oh, thank you for your help,' Mrs Gillies replied graciously. 'Come along girls,' and she swept along the marble floor as if on rollers. They left the foyer section and moved along through a corridor which was more like a museum gallery and Shelley marvelled at the wealth of writing talent. Each side of the seemingly endless passageway was framed pictures the full length of the walls, all perfectly lined up in sequence. Each photograph depicted the famous authors of the day in glossy poses. Shelley recognised them all straight away. Benjamin Crogg of the famous 'Perfect Line' mysteries, Lana Bowmont, author of fifteen novels on the 'Geraldene Masters' adventures and Clifton Withers, author of the comical 'Wizbank Swing' novels. The list went on and on. Katie followed behind her, knowing some of the famous people, but not as well as her best friend did. Shelley stopped for a moment and gazed in awe. A picture of an odd-looking fellow with wild, beady eyes and a mop of brown hair, looking quite wicked in his pose. This was Niloc Snosrap, the writer Shelley had come to see. Katie also became filled with an overwhelming glee. Hopefully he was signing his new novel 'How deep is the Hole' and Shelley was really hoping to get a signed copy.

'Come on, Shell. We're slowing up the others,' Katie interrupted Shelley's daydream with a whisper. Shelley blinked her eyes and brought herself back to reality. She took one last reluctant look then strolled on. Soon they were at the main event, the Exhibition Hall. There were no doors here, just an archway, and a vast area encompassing at least a quarter of a mile. Inside the archway, positioned like sentries, were two flagpoles. At the top, displayed on stiffened flag boards, were the words "World Book Day" emblazoned in blue capital letters on a yellow background. Everyone lined up in readiness to enter the hall.

'Wow,' was all that Shelley could spill from her lips. She studied the flags for a few moments and something else took her interest. Beyond the flags were different sections with advertising hoardings promoting new and popular books and authors. There were queues of people in different parts of the hall, waiting patiently for their autographed novels. Popular authors were buried under piles of perfectly stacked towers of reading matter, but it wasn't this sight that pulled her interest. High above the busy floor line was a very strange sight indeed. Suspended and tethered by six steel ropes was a book. Not just any old book, but a book around the size of a house. Its body was tilted as if ready to read, with opened and exposed giant printed pages. 'Enjoy Reading' was advertised on it in gigantic bold lettering that spilled over the two pages. Attached at the top and draped down the centre spine of the book was a black bookmark ribbon. This hung precariously over the edge and dangled freely over the crowd. It was a sight Shelley had never seen before and her eyes bulged from their sockets. The book was set dead centre of the hall, and there was a magnitude of activity to get through first; to be able to eye it from beneath. Shelley urgently and excitedly threaded her way through the eager crowds with her friend in tow.

'Slow down, Shell... there's plenty of time, you know,' Katie pleaded as she grabbed Shelley's cardigan and was pulled along. Shelley slowed her pace and panted heavily. The rest of her class had by now poured into the hall and gone their separate ways. Some didn't have any interest in books, like the Scrag Girls, so they went to the activities section, where they could mess around with interactive games and novelties.

Shelley saw another sign entitled "Victoria Scoggins best selling children's author signing today". This author sat voraciously signing copies of her new work, whilst a rather fidgety old lady with wide, sinister, staring eyes waited impatiently. To Shelley's left, another plaque, on another table, read "Janet F. Prendergast" and the words "Quiet Life" appeared in smaller letters underneath, but no sign of Shelley's favourite author yet. 'Where is he? Where is he?' she mouthed under her breath, getting a little agitated.

Katie noticed him first, but was unable to speak. Shelley followed her eye line and her heart stopped! There he was - Niloc Snosrap, and only feet away. They could almost touch him, but the queue was like a mile long and getting longer by the second. It was so exciting, but for a moment something else took Shelley's attention, it was a little further along. A glint of light reflected from a glass-panelled cabinet. There were a throng of people in front of it, but the cabinet containing The Object was higher than even the tallest person's head. It was definitely a book, of course it was. She shook her head and scolded herself for thinking it could be anything else in a book exhibition. She felt a familiar, violent tugging at her shoulder and she begrudgingly turned around to hear Katie shouting at her.

'Shell... if we don't get a move on we'll never get a signed copy. The line is getting longer.' Katie's eyes were blazing.

'I'll be there in a minute, you go,' Shelley replied ominously.

'What? Without you?' There was a pause for a moment and with that Katie released her grip and walked off in temper. Shelley tried to muster up some breath to call after her, but couldn't find the energy. Anyway, at that moment she was more interested in that display case. The thought of making up with her friend filled her mind. I'll let her cool off for a while, she reasoned, and then she went to satisfy her curiosity. This was way too mysterious to miss.

Chapter 2

Baby Creatures

Outside, another coach came to a stop. The teachers got off and started counting the pupils as they exciedly swarmed into the coach park.

'Twenty-seven, twenty-eight,' Mr Fairbourne mouthed the numbers to himself in an extremely focused manner.

'Can we go now, sir?' one boy called out, bored at waiting around for all the preliminaries to cease. 'It's cold,' he said stamping his feet with impatience.

'Patience, Thomas, patience.' Mr Fairbourne frowned at the boy. 'Now, where was I? Ah, yes, twenty- nine, thirty.' Mr Fairbourne was a tall, elderly teacher with tired eyes and a dry sense of humour, but stood for no shenanigans.

'Filpot, Laurence, stop messing about or no one will be going anywhere.' The voice of Mr Granger growled from behind. The two boys turned away from both teachers, rolled their eyes, and pulled faces at each other.

'Now then, form an orderly line and follow me. Mr Granger will be at the back, so behave.' The troop of pupils followed their teacher, chatting excitedly as they entered the huge building.

'Excuse me, please...' Mr Fairbourne boomed. 'We must meet back here at three o'clock and no later. Enjoy yourselves everyone, and behave.' He shot a deliberate stare at certain children that he knew were mischievous. They sifted through to enter the vast area that was the Exhibition Hall, and soon everyone mixed with the crowds. Mr Fairbourne wandered along the walkway with his colleague Mr Granger. Suddenly something caught his attention.

'I'm going over here, Reg. I'll see you later,' he told Mr Granger.

Meanwhile, still with the guilty feeling of splitting up from Katie, Shelley strolled over to the attraction. On closer inspection, she saw the cabinet was lit from sparkling rays of light that filtered through the glass and bathed its contents in a warm orange and yellow glow. In fact, it reminded her of the display cases in a jewellery shop window, but on a much grander scale. The light emanated from directly above, and she gasped, realising the source. The laser lighting was fixed to the giant book display that was high above her head. She wanted to get a better look at the glass box, and tried to penetrate the dense array of people. There were school children and adults mixed tightly together, and not one would allow her in. A gap, though, did appear eventually, and she took her chance and pushed through. Now she was within the inner circle, there was more chance to thread through the tightly knit pack of onlookers. She stepped forward and craned her neck, gazing at the almost hypnotic bars of light that locked onto their target. Paying too much attention above, and not totally focusing on where she was heading, she tripped over the first person that she tried to pass, and crash- landed on the hard-ribbed carpet. After that, Shelley found it difficult to stand back up, so she spent most of the time on the floor, climbing through the maze of people's legs, to the annoyance of their owners. Eventually, and with a determined effort, and lack of oxygen, the teenager bore through, until she was nearly at the front. As the last of the crowd parted, she stood up and took a huge intake of breath, with a thankful smile. This turned to a look of utter disgust as in mid-suction, she realised that someone had farted! Shelley fanned her hand madly in front of her nose to disperse the foul odour, which reminded her of 'gone-off' boiled cabbage. Her face screwed up and her eyes squinted under the intense pong, but it was forgotten in an instant... There it was... 'Secrets of Time' by Thomas Nigglesforth. It appeared to float inside the casing, and Shelley was mesmerised.

'I've read about this book,' she said aloud, and quickly realised that people were staring. She wisely kept the rest of the conversation in her head. It was in a magazine, I'm sure it was, she thought. She eased closer to touch the glass, but was soon ousted back by two grim-looking security guards; they looked as if they were waiting to pummel someone into pulp. She cowered down, there were a few sniggers from the crowd behind, and Shelley's face reddened with embarrassment. She soon shrugged it off and stared again, in awe. The book itself was leather-bound, and in a state of disrepair. Inscribed on the cover, in tarnished gold lettering, were the title and the name of the author. The writing was very fanciful, with swirls of gold intertwined and almost illegible, but there was something else. The book title was at the top, and the author's name was at the bottom, but halfway down was a beautifully designed piece of jewellery. It protruded out from the centre of the cover. It was a brilliant, blue diamond, mounted on top of a patterned web of gold; the size of a coffee coaster. Shelley could not take her eyes off it. A card on a glass plinth displayed the book's picture and a brief history:

This book, 'Secrets of Time', and its author, Thomas Nigglesforth, are a complete mystery. The book appeared in Tellington University Library in 1994. No one has any information aboutThomas Nigglesforth, and the book itself has been carefully scrutinised by experts, but has yielded no clues. Why, suddenly, such an expensive item had been left there, is still a mystery. The University will keep the book until it is reclaimed by its owner. The current estimated value of the book is One Million Pounds.

Shelley's eyes widened, and her mouth dropped open. It also went on to say that the book itself had a magnificent historical value, but the diamond on its own was worth three quarters of a million.

'Wow,' the words tumbled off her tongue. Still reeling from the shock, she felt herself being shoved forward. Soon more people came to see the spectacle, and she was pushed to one side, and away from the exhibit. She found herself once more beside the Niloc Snosrap table, but this time, to her devastation, the queue was enormous. She looked down the line, but couldn't see Katie anywhere.

Her eyes were once more drawn to the famous book, and the throng of people suffocating it, but this time, something else was there! Shelley couldn't believe her eyes at first, so she rubbed them vigorously, opened them wide and took another look.

There was a small group of 'people' standing on the outskirts of the crowd. They were little people, strange people, nothing like she'd ever seen before. She could see at least eight of them, but these weren't ordinary people by any means. They stood about four feet tall, and all wore black body-hugging suits, the same as skiers wore, almost. Not only this, but they all appeared to be bald, and as if that wasn't enough, their skin was blue in colour. One turned to look in Shelley's direction, its face resembled the features of a baby. Each had a round, chubby face, with a dinky nose and thin lips, but each wore a sinister expression. Shelley found this fascinating, and screwed up her eyes to make sure she wasn't seeing things. They also appeared to be trying to penetrate the crowd, as she just had, but they couldn't get through.

The other strange thing that amazed the schoolgirl was the fact that nobody else seemed to notice them. Passers-by wandering through the exhibits, people queuing for autographs, no one seemed to notice this small and strange band of creatures. But she could see them, as plain as day.

Every now and then, the blue people pushed gently through any gap they could find; but although they tried to tease their way in, failed miserably. Shelley looked on as they formed a group, and dropped their heads down in a sort of team conference, and then lifted up and suddenly dispersed as a loose group, but all going in the same direction. Filled with curiosity, she felt compelled to follow. Considering they couldn't push through a dense crowd of people, they weren't slow in weaving through the lighter population of the hall. Shelley darted after them, still wondering why no one could see them. She eventually caught up to see the last of them disappear behind one of the doors marked "Staff Only". Quickly, without causing attention to herself, she moved up to the door entrance.

'What am I doing?' she whispered, and her stomach tightened. She gave a swift, nervous glance around to make sure no one was watching, took a deep breath, and slipped inside unnoticed. From the brightly lit hall, she was now encompassed in semi-darkness. A cool breeze fanned through the corridor, she waited a moment, and strained to hear. She couldn't see much of anything. They can't be far ahead, she thought. Her eyes gradually grew accustomed to the dimness, and with a renewed confidence, she moved farther in. Ahead, though, there was the soft amber glow of a light. The mellow beam cast its sombre rays along the passageway and ended with spots of yellow that reflected onto the shape of a staircase, in the same way cinema steps would be illuminated. The stairway itself was a metal framework that ascended into the eaves. She reached out and felt for a hand rail and sure enough there it was. She surged upwards and quickly noticed the noise she was making. With every step came an echoed clanking from her shoes, hitting the metal surface, which also vibrated through to her fingertips. She didn't want to alert the creatures, so she stopped and tried again, softer this time. But it didn't make any difference, the sound still gave her presence away, so she picked up pace.

It had been a while since she laid eyes on the blue people, and she worried that she might actually be chasing ghosts. Her breathing became heavier and her legs were starting to ache. By the time she reached the top, her lungs felt like two full supermarket shopping bags, and her legs felt three times their normal size. Her cheeks were flushed, and the joints of her inner arms hurt. Awkwardly, she pulled herself onto the platform at the top and collapsed onto her back. Time was of the essence now, so she pushed her aching body upright, and quickly peered over a partition safety barrier... and dived back down to hide. Still panting, she placed both hands on the top of the barrier, and gingerly lifted herself to eye level.

From her vantage point, Shelley could see the whole Exhibition Hall in all of its glory. From this height, the people scurrying round below resembled bees in a hive. The magnificent book display hung open below her; it looked as if it was itching to be read by any passing giant. She looked along the centre pages, and saw the blue people she had been chasing, hanging over the place where the bookmark drooped. Shelley tilted her head and peered underneath the spine of the book.

From this angle she could see a slender length of shimmering thread being lowered over the cabinet. The same cabinet with the limited edition book inside. On the end of the string, suspended in mid-air, was one of the creatures. Shelley was fascinated by this and watched in curious silence. The others lowered the small creature until he was hovering about half a metre above the top of the book. It was amazing to Shelley that no one, not the guards, the onlookers, the crowds of autograph hunters... no one had noticed anything happening! The creature reached out his hand, and seemed to melt his arm through the glass as if as reaching through fog. The blue creature then gripped the book, still with an audience of people watching, but not seeing, and lifted it away. Shelley almost called out, but when she looked into the cabinet, the book was apparently still there! But the creature was holding it in his hand, and the others were pulling him back up. What is going on? she thought. Things were happening so fast that Shelley didn't know what to do. The group of creatures was now all on the display together, with the book. They then made for the metal catwalk. One by one they filed along the steel walkway, all eight of them, with the last one carrying the stolen book.

In a fit of madness, Shelley lunged over the walkway and dived onto the last creature, but missed him completely, and fell helplessly onto the giant book display itself, unnoticed by the creatures as they made their getaway. Still travelling at a fair pace, she slid down the centre channel and tipped over the edge. She tried to scream, but her throat was so dry only a squeak came out. Instinctively she grasped at whatever she could, and grabbed the tail end of the bookmark ribbon. She hung on for all she was worth, and luckily for her, noticed the ribbon had horizontal loops heavily sewn into the material. So she pulled herself up, using the loops like rungs on a ladder, and eventually clambered onto the page. She turned after a moment and looked down over the edge, expecting to find a crowd of people looking up at her, but no one seemed to notice her either. Perhaps they were all too busy with the event.

Still shaking, Shelley climbed up the remainder of the ribbon aiming to stop at the top. When she was only inches from the top of the page, she gradually eased her head over the edge and peered across. There was a gap of about ten feet between the end of the book and the metal platform, which joined onto a narrow gangplank bridging the two. Beside that was the drop, all the way down to the hall floor, and from where she was it looked a very long way down indeed.

Her breathing became rapid again, and her heart

pumped hard against her chest. She was now standing with the tips of her shoes overhanging the edge of the book. From the time it took to climb to the top of the giant page, she could just make out the last of the blue creatures disappearing down a flight of stairs. She knew it would be too late to catch up with them if she dawdled any longer. So she mustered up all her courage and stepped forward onto the gangplank, with her eyes firmly shut. Without thinking and before she knew it, Shelley was back on the platform, to her utter amazement. She once more chased after them.

Finally she made it to the stairway on the other side. Without stopping, she dashed down the long flight of metal stairs, and at the bottom there was... nothing! No blue creatures, no book, and no idea as to where they had gone. It was semi-dark once more, so Shelley fumbled until she came to yet another door, and through that she was back out into the Exhibition Hall, but on the other side this time. Everything seemed normal. The queues were still trailing way back, and the excitement buzzed through the air. Shelley could see Katie in the middle of the line of people, so she waved, but Katie was still sulking and didn't return the friendly gesture. Did she just imagine all that had happened? Just then a flood of officials and security guards burst through the crowds and surrounded the glass display case. The inside of the cabinet was indeed empty! She hadn't imagined it, but who was going to believe her story. A full-scale alert was taking place. Uniformed staff examined the empty glass box. Throughout all the commotion, Shelley noticed something happening by the "Staff Only" doorway. There, tucking something into the inside of his suit, was another of the blue creatures. Without thinking, she snaked her way urgently through the confused body of people that were being herded to one side of the building by security guards. Shelley eventually made it to the door, and pushed her way through.

Inside was a sight that blew her mind. A circular hatch was slowly closing inside the corridor. In the seconds she had to think what to do, she realised the round door wasn't fixed to anything, but suspended above the floor. She juggled the thoughts in her mind of 'going or staying', but just leapt straight inside. The hatch eventually closed and melted away, leaving a pool of residue on the floor in its place. Another lookout, a single blue creature, came down the stairway and, having missed the doorway closing, immersed himself in the purple liquid. He vanished, leaving the jelly-like substance in mid-evaporation.

Chapter 3

The Other Side

Shelley landed with a thud, on a soft, damp surface and winced in disgust. There was a smell that could only be described as horrid. The soft ground she'd landed on was brown and squishy and was fast staining her clothes. She lifted her head, and looked straight ahead. There they were, the group of blue people she had so vigorously pursued, and they were only a short distance ahead, oblivious to their pursuer. She then noticed where she was, deep inside a dirty, grey-walled tunnel that swept far into the distance, and lit by oblong lights, set in sequence along the walls. For a moment, she felt as though she was being watched from behind, but was so confused that she quickly forgot the idea. I can't go any further, I must get back to the exhibition, she reasoned inside her head. All I need to do is to climb back through the hatch, get cleaned up, and try and explain what's happened.

Once she'd set things straight in her mind, she turned around. The exit wasn't there, right behind her as it should have been, but was sailing away into the distant tunnel, and vanished, just like a flame being extinguished! She felt sick, and saliva filled her mouth, which she most unladylike, spat out. All she could see behind her now was a long, empty tunnel that veered out of sight. The feeling of being watched was unfounded, as there was no one there, just an empty tunnel. A cold chill of loneliness filled her whole being, and she began to sob at the thought of being stuck inside, who-knows-where? And not knowing if she could find her way out set her into a flood of tears. Her wailing amplified throughout the tunnel. It alerted the small group of creatures, who immediately turned. She eventually wiped her streaming eyes and opened them again, only to be confronted by the very creatures she'd followed there.

They looked angry; their eyes blazed yellow, with tiny black specks at their centres, fixed terrifyingly on her. They were grunting and muttering amongst themselves. Slowly they moved closer, and began screeching such a piercing and painful tone, that Shelley was petrified and covered her ears to muffle the excruciatingly high pitch. Something touched her fingers, and she let out a tremendous scream. She threw up her hands to push whatever it was away. The baby creatures surged forward, and in the same instant, something gripped her wrists tightly. She struggled, but was yanked up into the air, and her slim, light frame lifted through the ceiling. She was dragged over a cold, rough surface. Whatever had grabbed her let her go just as quickly. Shelley curled up into a ball, and screwed her eyes tightly shut. She lay on the stone floor and was afraid to open her eyes, terrified of what she might find should she dare to open them.

Nothing happened! So gradually she gently relaxed and opened her eyes. There, in front of her, was a boy of about the same age as herself. He was twisting a wheel in a clockwise motion, until it locked a lid into place. He must have pulled me through, she thought.

'There, that should do it,' he said, and puffed out his cheeks with satisfaction. 'They shouldn't get through there in a hurry,' the boy mumbled to himself, and sat down. He turned to face her, and for the first time she could see him. It wasn't full daylight where they were situated, but it was brighter than the tunnel. His hair was black and unkempt and flopped over his eyebrows. He had brown eyes, red cheeks and a stubby nose. He gave her a steely glare. 'What were you thinking? Are you crazy? You can't challenge Plogs,' he ranted. Shelley was dumbfounded, and she peered back with her mouth wide open, but nothing came out. She didn't know what to say or do, and began to sob again. The boy felt a twang of guilt. He hadn't seen a girl for quite a while in his world, and it felt strange to him. 'What are you doing here?' he pressed, though more gently this time.

'I... I don't know,' she blabbed honestly, and tried to make sense of all that had happened to her in the last hour or so. She felt confused and cold sitting on a concrete floor and was a little angry with herself for getting into the position that she now found herself in.

'Well, you couldn't have chosen a more dangerous place to be,' the boy reported with conviction.

'Why? What part of Tellington am I in?' she enquired.

'Tellington? What are you talking about? I've never heard of that place.' The boy looked back at Shelley with a puzzled expression.

'I have come from an exhibition in Tellington,' she persisted, but the teenage boy looked confused at her words.

'I've got no idea what you are talking about, we are in Scarrat Town,' he said.

Shelley was lost for a moment, then chirped positively, 'How do I get back, then? Is there a bus I can take?' Her face changed from a confused disgruntled look into a stern one. The boy stared back blankly.

'What's a bus?' he asked with a feeling of uncertainty.

'What's a bus? Are you winding me up or what?' she raged, her nerves frayed. 'Everyone knows what a bus is. This place is really strange. Look, I'm dirty, smelly and tired, and I've got to get home.' She calmed down a little and said, 'I'm sorry, thank you for rescuing me.' She had always been taught to be polite. 'What's your name?' Shelley continued, in a calmer refrain.

'Kevin, what's yours?' he replied.

'I'm Shelley,' she said.

'How did you get here?' he asked curiously.

'There was a round doorway, and I climbed through it, and followed those blue people,' she said as she tugged at her damp clothes and tried to tease her hair into some shape.

'The blue people, as you call them, are called Plogs, and they are very dangerous, believe me,' he said, and pushed his hair out of his eyes. She closed her eyes in regret when she realised that her glasses were missing.

'Oh, no,' she sighed.

'What's the matter?' He could see she was in torment.

'I lost my glasses in the tunnel. They must have fallen off in the confusion.'

'I can't open the hatch back up, otherwise they'll capture us. Can you see without them?' he sympathised.

'Yeah, I only need them for reading and computers really.' Shelley felt a little more cheerful, 'But mum will kill me when she finds out.'

'I'm not going to even ask what a computer is.' He smiled a wide grin and asked, 'Why were you following them?'

'They stole a valuable book from the exhibition, and I only wanted to try and get it back.'

'Shadrack Scarrat has been asking about a book, I've heard rumours.' Kevin drifted off into deep thought.

'Who is Shadrack Scarrat?' Shelley probed, and stood up from the concrete floor.

'He runs this place. He's evil and ruthless and not to be trusted... he'll suck you in, if you're not careful,' Kevin said with a real fear. 'Anyway, we can't stay here, it won't be long before they discover a way into this derelict warehouse.' And as the words left his mouth, they sent a shiver right through Shelley's body.

'We'd better leave, then, if we're not safe here,' Shelley said.

'They won't find us that easily, Shell.' Kevin said her name without thinking, and felt awkward at saying it.

'You don't understand, they can slip through solid glass,' she said with wide, staring eyes. 'I've seen them.'

'I know, but don't worry, they have the power to move through solid objects... but only if they can see through them.' He smiled for a moment. 'I've seen them do it, but if something is shielded by a metal cover, or too solid to penetrate, they lose confidence in themselves, like now,' he concluded.

'But how do these Plogs appear and disappear?'

Shelley probed curiously.

'I'm not really sure, but I have seen them carrying some kind of device,' Kevin recollected. Shelley for the first time since leaving the exhibition felt some hope of getting back.

'That's it then,' she announced. 'I need that device.'

'Oh, yeah,' Kevin blurted sarcastically. 'We'll just walk up to one of the Plogs and take one then.' Shelley felt hurt at his attitude, and began to walk across the deserted warehouse alone.

'Where are you going?... all right, all right, I was only joking. We'll find a way,' he called out, and chased after her. 'You're very easy to upset,' he said, sneering. 'Shelley, Shell, wait, you don't even know where you're going.'

She turned and smiled. 'You'll help me then?'

Kevin then knew he'd been had, and been caught by the oldest trick in the book... female cunning. 'Yeah, all right.' He gave her a long, silent stare, widened his face to a grin, and scratched his head.

They walked through the warehouse, with Shelley still attempting to engage in conversation as she continued with her questions. But Kevin wasn't listening, and was concentrating on escape.

'Look, if we carry on this way, we may get to the end before the Plogs exit the tunnel,' Kevin announced with a spark of enthusiasm. He stepped ahead, and tried to remember which way he had to go to cut them off.

Light poured into the old warehouse through dusty and cobwebbed windows. Some windows were broken, leaving splintered remains that crunched underfoot.

There were parts of the roof which had collapsed and the sheeting was strewn onto the ground. There were various obstacles, wooden boxes that had been long broken open, leaving dangerous, nailed planks of wood lying around. Small piles of empty sacks were discarded, previously ravaged by some intruder or another, long ago, by the amount of dust settled upon them. Shelley gazed up through the holes in the roof and studied the sky. Menacing charcoal clouds threatened a storm and the sun seemed to have abandoned its place. She was so busy looking up and not looking where she was going that she fell head first into a chute.

Kevin heard something, and stopped. He turned to see what the problem was, but Shelley was nowhere in sight. He waited for a moment, trying to figure out where she had gone. She was right behind me a minute ago, he thought. He went pale, and scurried around looking for her.

'Shelley, Shell, where are you?' Kevin called nervously, to no avail. 'Are you hiding? Come on, we haven't time to muck about.' Only the echoed footsteps of the boy shuffling around the warehouse filled the air. A lump came to his throat and his heart beat hard. He stopped abruptly, and realised that unless he stopped panicking, he was going nowhere fast. He stood quietly, and listened. The wind was still hissing through the windows, and the scurrying of a rodent far-off somewhere pulled at his concentration. But wait! What was that? He closed his eyes and concentrated even harder, with all the determination he could muster. Somewhere, there was a muffled, rubbing sound. It didn't sound like a rat, or an animal of any sort, this time. It must be Shelley, he thought. 'Try and help me to find you, Shell!' he shouted, in echo.

'Mumph... mumph... blam... bloo, bloo,' the mumbled reply came back.

'That's it, keep calling,' he said with a new excitement, and he moved faster, to where he thought the sound was emitting. But he was a little too vigorous in his rescue attempt, and he also fell down into the same hole!

'AAARGH!' Kevin slid down the winding chute at great speed, not having time to stop himself. He landed with a muffled thump, in the same spot that Shelley had just been. He sank into a soft landing, which seemed to engulf him and pull him down below the surface. It was itchy, dark and hot, and the air was thin. Kevin began to quickly fight back. He clawed, and wrestled his way to the surface, and broke through. With a huge puff of wind, and with a massive relief, he pulled himself out.

'Shelley, where are you?' he screamed frantically. He could just make out a hand on one side of a sea of sacking. He wriggled and manoeuvred to the spot where his new friend was sinking fast into a pile of brown Hessian sacks. 'Hold on, I've got you,' he said, reaching out his hand, and digging inside the hairy material, until he clasped his hand around her clammy limp wrist. She was suffocating, and he didn't have much time; she had already been under a little while. The floppy sacking pulled her down like quicksand and made it really difficult to keep hold. He pulled, and pulled again, and peeled away the layers, until finally he felt her elbow and shoulders. He hooked his arms under both her armpits and pulled like his life depended upon it. He heaved with one last jerk, and out she popped and landed on top of him. Her limp body slumped over his and didn't move.

Kevin panicked, and quickly flipped her over onto her back. Shelley's cheeks were bright red, and her arms and face were rubbed raw with the abrasive texture of the Hessian. She wasn't moving and he was all fingers and thumbs. He didn't know whether to loosen her clothing, or shake her, or what the heck should he do? His mind raced. He lifted his hands and tugged at his hair. Instinct took over and he slapped her face with a crack. With that, her blue eyes blinked open, and she gasped for air. Kevin was just about to raise his hand and slap her again.

'DON'T-YOU-DARE!' she burst and sat up, rubbing her cheek. 'What are you doing?' She gave him a piercing glare, and in relief, Kevin flopped on his back and breathed hard. Shelley regrouped her thoughts and fitted the pieces back together. She stared into space until her eyes flickered, and she turned to Kevin.

'I remember now, the fall, sinking into sacking, and I could have... I could have died.' She smiled at him sweetly. 'Thank you, Kevin. You saved me.'

But Kevin was oblivious to her compliment. He was already up and searching for a way out. They were both perched on a vast pile of old sacking at the bottom of a shaft. He scanned the walls vigorously; they were too high, with no offer of footholds or grips of any kind. So, there was no chance of getting out the same way as they had got in. He bit his lip in annoyance and sucked air through his teeth. Shelley was still babbling in the background, but Kevin was in too deep a thought to hear any of it. If they threw the old sacks down here when they were empty, how did they re-use them to fill them back up? He rolled the thought over and over in his mind.

'What are you looking for, Kevin?' Shelley asked.

'Wha...oh, a way out, what do you think?' he answered abrasively, still annoyed at falling down into a trap that he should have been prepared for.

'I was only asking,' she said grumpily. 'What's that?' She then pointed to one side of the sack pile. Kevin followed the direction of her finger, and could see what she was seeing. Although the whole place was obscured with bags, there was something poking through the top thin layer of Hessian. He fumbled his way to the source, and once he'd removed the loose bagging... he could see a metal bar! It was connected to what looked like a hatch, or a door of some kind, and a bead of light outlined the top. Kevin's eyes grew wide with excitement and his smile banished the gloom. With both hands, he gripped the latch and pulled. It was obvious that it hadn't been moved for many years, it was jammed! He realised that by pulling the bar free, the hatch would open outwards.

'Aarrgh!' he cried with frustration, and he wrenched and wrestled with the stubborn bar. Shelley stood behind him, and grinned without him seeing her. He didn't take much to get wound up either.

'I'll give you a hand.' Shelley moved to his side and gripped a small section of the bar.

'Right, after three we pull,' he said commandingly, and took a hard grip. 'One...'

'Wow... hold on, hold on. Do we pull when you've finished saying two? Or when you actually start to say three? Or at the end of three?' Shelley asked, confused.

Kevin looked on in utter disbelief, screwed up his eyes and thought, is she real? 'Look,' he said trying to bring some normality into his boyish world. 'I'll say one, then two, and then three, and after I have finished saying three, we pull together, all right?' He peered deep into her eyes patronisingly.

'All right,' she answered sulkily, and gave a slight nod.

'One… two… three.' And with that, they both heaved with all their strength, and with the intense pulling power of both… it loosened, and they felt a slight jolt. They gave a huge sigh as Shelley let go, and Kevin gripped it himself again. He pulled, but although it had loosened, it wasn't loose enough. Kevin looked at Shelley and nodded in a motion to try again.

'Come on, Shell,' he said, and they both took hold once more. 'One… two… three.' Again they pulled, with Shelley feeling a little weaker this time. It wasn't moving, so Shelley pooled all her resources and tensed. This time it gave way to the sheer surprise of both teenagers. They fell back, and the door opened to its fullest, under the intense pressure of the sacks. But it wasn't a small hatch doorway at all; it was a much larger door. The contents of the pit poured out like custard from a jug, and in a cloud of dust, out popped two tons of sacking and two very disorientated teenagers. Shelley landed on her side, and Kevin landed upside down. They rolled over and faced each other, with dazed expressions. The corridor where they had landed was brighter than the sacking chute, and light shone through from the holes in the ceiling. The dust filtered away, leaving two grey-covered figures. When they realised their predicament, they began to laugh out loud. Kevin hadn't laughed in a long time, especially a full belly laugh. But he soon stopped and became serious again. Shelley stopped also, and could tell the mood had changed.

'We haven't time to lark around, Shell. We must get that book. I think I know where we are. Follow me. We can cut off the Plogs before they leave the tunnel,' he said smartly, his expression filled with concentration, and he moved up the passage with knowledgeable intent. Shelley climbed out of her sack bedding and hurriedly chased after him. He was by now steaming ahead like a train.

'Wait for me,' she called anxiously.

'Sshhh,' he whispered. 'If they're near, they'll hear us,' he hissed, pressing his index finger to his lips, and she said no more, tagging quietly behind.

It began to get dark again, but before too long the semi-darkness of the underground passage was streaked in bright light again.

'Ah, I thought so,' he said, studying the area. 'You see here, Shell? This is where those sacks we landed in were hoisted back up onto ground level and loaded into wagons, and were taken away to get refilled.' Sure enough, there was another shaft, but this time there was a long rope with a kind of basket fitted to the end, like the workings of an old well. The equipment was long since worn by time; the rope was rotten, and the wooden basket had holes in it from damp rot.

'Can we get out this way?' Shelley asked innocently.

Kevin looked at her with puzzled eyes. He could see she was genuine, in the fact that she didn't know the rope would break if any weight was placed upon it now.

'No, Shell. We need to find the Plogs and get you out of here, and if we carry on in this direction, I think we can head them off,' he said not wanting to make her feel stupid.

'What happens when we do catch up with them?' she asked blankly.

Kevin was not sure about that himself. 'I don't know. We'll have to see what we can do when we get there,' he said uncomfortably. 'Let's go, we haven't much time.'

Chapter 4

Not Far Behind

Katie felt awkward about not acknowledging her friend, and began to slowly lose her stubbornness. She looked around, but couldn't see her. Well, she was there a minute ago, where had she gone? she pondered. There was also something strange happening generally in the hall itself, a disturbance of some kind was taking place. Some officials rushed past, and from the grimace on their faces it didn't look good. Up ahead of the queue and past the authors' table, she could see the panic instilled in the faces of the security people inspecting the cabinet. She squinted, and saw what they were looking at - the cabinet was empty! That's where Shelley was headed when I left her, she thought. I'm sure there was something inside it. Why didn't I take notice?

'Oh, someone's stolen that famous book. Look, the cabinet's empty,' one tallish woman commented a little farther up the queue.

'That's the one in the paper, isn't it, the one that's worth about a zillion pounds?' another short, plump lady exclaimed in front of her.

'No, not a zillion pounds, a million pounds. It's here in my paper,' a rather important-looking man in a sharp, black suit interrupted.

'Why is it worth that much, anyway? It's only a book,' the original woman asked curiously.

'Here, look?' continued the black-suited man, showing his newspaper to his curious audience. 'There's a precious stone set in the cover.' He folded the paper in half and the onlookers studied it.

'Wow, no wonder they're looking so worried,' Katie blurted, and everyone turned to look at her. Her cheeks reddened when she realised that what she was actually thinking she'd said instead. When they'd all turned away again, she began to get concerned about Shelley. How could someone have stolen something in full view of the crowds? And where was Shelley? There was a lot of confusion now and worried faces were swarming into the exhibition. Suddenly, security staff appeared from everywhere and started moving in on the crowds of gawping onlookers. Katie felt isolated from her friends and teachers, which frightened her. She panicked as people heaved and pushed from every side. All the authors that she could see had stopped signing books and were caught up in the choppy sea of confusion. People in her queue were also nervously whispering and muttering to one another.

Katie frantically scanned round the hall for a glimpse of Mrs Gillies or Miss Shanks or even the Scrag Girls, anyone familiar. It was ironic, but for the first time in her life she really needed her snooty deputy head to show herself. She also noticed that all the authors from each of the tables were being escorted out through a side doorway. 'What makes them so special?' she said, grinding her teeth in annoyance.

She stood silently and did a complete sweep of the room, taking in all that she could see. It was difficult with all the movement that was taking place, but wait, her body tensed, and she eased forward a little, when she suddenly saw Shelley slip through an exit door to one side of the hall. Her heart raced as she sucked in air and frantically waved her arms.

'Shelley! Shelley!' Katie called out, but as quickly as she'd made visual contact Shelley had gone. Katie knew she had to get to her friend and find out what was happening.

'Attention... attention. Everyone stay calm. If you will take instruction from our security people and line up, everything will be over and we can carry on with the exhibition.' The calm, posh voice washed over the crowd like a slow tumbling wave rolling toward the shore. There wasn't going to be much time before she would be caught up in the gathering process. So she ducked down and melted away inside a large gang of excited looking Japanese tourists who were flashing away anxiously with their long-lens cameras. There was a lot more activity than they were expecting at a book signing, and they loved it. They stared at the suspicious-looking schoolgirl, then nodded and laughed to one another as she wove between them.

Totally unnoticed by the imploding security, Katie turned this way and that, always aware that the net was ever tightening around her. She breathed hard, and her hands were clammy. This was a new quest for her and the adrenaline-rush excited her. With the rapid breathing came tightness in her chest; she felt as though she might pass out. Finally, there in front of her, was the emergency door that Shelley had used.

'Please keep all exits clear,' the faceless voice echoed from the speaker above her head. That made things worse, and Katie gulped a large mouthful of air and stood right outside the doorway. What should she do? Shelley's in there, she thought. She began trembling, and beads of perspiration strayed down each of her cheeks. *I can't do this.* She struggled with her conscience. She was panicking, and her heart was doing a drum roll as she bit her bottom lip. She had thought deeply about it, and decided against the idea. *Shelley's probably all right,* she thought. *I'll go back and find the others, and she'll probably turn up there.* But with that thought, fate took a different role. As she was about to turn away, a large teenager came barging past with a security guard hot on his heels. The boy knocked her straight through the fire exit door. Katie tumbled and landed in a pool of purple slime that covered a small portion of the immediate floor inside. Her hands and face were wet and her clothes sodden in the smelly gooey substance.

'Yuck!' she shrieked, and lifted herself to her knees. 'What is this stuff?' It was semi-darkness inside the corridor, and she could just make out the gel that was soaking through the rest of her clothes and body at a rate of knots. The slime dripped on her face and into her ears and mouth. Frantically she tried to wipe it off, but it seemed to have a life of its own. It was slowly covering every part of her body. She poked out her tongue in disgust. It tasted vile! It also began to tingle, just like 'pins and needles.' Katie looked at her hands in the dim light. Suddenly the shock made her almost stop breathing. Her hands were still tingling, but also turning transparent. It swallowed her up whole and pulled her in. Katie opened her gel-filled mouth to force a scream, but it didn't happen. Before the sound had left her lips, everything went black!

With her mouth still wide open, and her eyes tight shut, she belted out a high pitched screech. When things fell silent, she gradually opened her eyes. Her hands, arms, legs and feet, were back to normal, the electric tingle had subsided, but now she was shocked into a full sense of dread. Where was she? She had just realised that, actually, she wasn't kneeling in a corridor anymore, but on a dirt road in the middle of an open space. She shivered as a cold wind whipped up a mini dust cloud. She shielded her eyes from the stinging grit that it tossed around. A deep sense of loss and isolation welled up inside, bringing back memories when she was eight and had been left behind in the fairground unable to find her parents. She began to cry. Large, bulbous tears poured down her dirty cheeks, streaking them with white stripes.

'Mum, where are you?' she sobbed, but her mother didn't come to her aid. Katie continued feeling sorry for herself for a while. She finally stopped, realising it didn't make any difference in this strange place.

Another thing she had noticed was the fact that the gooey stuff had also gone. The sky above was heavily grey and foreboding, to each side of the road trees and mountains rose into the distance. What was she doing here? And where was Shelley? She let out a shout.

'SHELLEY...' Her voice echoed across the distant hills and faded. She took a deep intake of breath and called out again. 'SHELLEY, ANSWER ME, WHERE ARE WE? You git!' There was bitterness in her voice this time, but her efforts were futile as once again her tones were lost in the hissing of the wind.

'Sod you, then,' she cursed, and turned from angry to sulky. She peered at the landscape, huffing and puffing with every movement.

She looked around. There was a large mound of

earth that stood out on a flat piece of ground, not far from where she knelt. And on the side that faced her, a round, rusty door depicted an entrance. On the ground in front of the doorway, imprinted into the thick dust, were footprints. These tiny, animal-like paw marks, led back from the hatch to exactly the same spot that she was kneeling. She studied them for a while, then got up and made her way over. She shivered again in the chilled wind and crossed her arms to keep warm. Why didn't she listen to mum and take her cardigan with her? Then she remembered with fondness her coat, hanging in the cloakroom. This gave her a brief feeling of regret. But that subsided, and she rubbed her arms vigorously. When she got closer, she could see that there were no handles or doorknobs to speak of, but only a pattern of dimples on the rusty metal surface. She leant against the door and pushed with all her body weight, which wasn't much, so of course, nothing moved. In temper she hammered it hard, and hurt the fleshy part of her palm. She winced and shook her hand violently, sucking air between her teeth.

'Damn it,' she cursed again. She eased off, and walked the few steps back to the road, still holding her injured hand and flexing her fingers. She stood dead centre and looked both ways - there was no distinction in either direction. The tracks were long and winding, and both disappeared out of sight. There were no buildings of any description, just road and country side. How on earth could she have come this far? Her hand was still throbbing, and this brought her back to reality. She weighed up her options and decided the way she wanted to go. Steadily, she began walking to nowhere in particular, shrugging off the throbbing of her aching limb. She started with a slow pace at first, and then with more determination quickened her stride. The sky looked threatening; the thickening clouds seemed to be watching her, following her. She walked for quite a while, taking in the surroundings; the landscape didn't change much. The hilly backdrop remained constant, and the length of the road relentless. Why aren't there any houses? Where are the people? All of these questions filled her tormented mind. Is Shelley okay? The road petered out, and Katie found herself descending a hill. This took her mind away from the scary thoughts. At the bottom of the hill the ground levelled off. The landscape changed to flatlands and a flicker of excitement filled her. There was a notice, a board with two wooden legs supporting it, which read, "Scarrat Town". She felt a warm feeling inside, as if everything was going to be all right. A smile lifted her otherwise worried-looking face.

'Thank goodness,' she said, as farther on up the road she could make out what looked like a small town. The shadow of evening was slowly pitching the land into darkness. All manner of thoughts raced through her mind. She could get food and drink. She hadn't noticed before because she had been upset, but she was really hungry and thirsty. A can of fizzy pop and a Danish pastry never looked so good, as the images flickered into her head. Her mouth began to water, and she slurped it back down. She could also get help, and find her way back home. It didn't look much from where she was standing, but there must be a phone... then she remembered her mobile. She reached for her shoulder to get it from her rucksack and closed her eyes. 'Oh brilliant,' she spat. Katie remembered that she and Shelley had been so excited about the exhibition and meeting their favourite author, that they had left them on the bus. She felt so annoyed she could have kicked herself. It was all too much and she couldn't contain her feelings any longer.

'Aaaargh,' she yelled, peering up into the ever darkening sky.

'Shh... quiet,' a voice interrupted her tantrum, and Katie stopped dead in her tracks! She stood motionless, and took deep shallow breaths. Who was that?

Chapter 5

On The Run

After walking for a short while, Kevin and Shelley came to a fork in the underground passageway. Kevin instinctively took the left corridor, but Shelley was unsure and stood at dead centre. The right path ascended into even slabs of stone, which gradually stepped higher and higher and disappeared into a spiral. A ray of light forced its way down from the outside. Its reflection curled the corner, and the wall's glassy surface held its bleached glow. To their left was a shorter route that led a little further along to a steel door with a hefty looking metal bar securing it. This is what caught Kevin's eye and why he chose that route in the first place. He made his way to it and was about to reach out and touch the latch when Shelley stopped him.

'Why are you going that way?' Shelley's questioned doubtfully, and her voice echoed through the empty stairway. Kevin turned and gave her a long deep stare.

'Why are you questioning me? I know where I'm going,' he growled menacingly, which scared Shelley a bit. He'd spent a long time on his own making his own decisions and found it hard to take criticism from someone else.

Shelley plucked up some courage, not wanting Kevin to get the better of her. 'All right,' she relented sharply, and in a louder tone said, 'I was only aski...'

Kevin cut her off mid-sentence. With his finger pressed firmly to his lips he hissed, 'Shhhh,' and he lowered his voice. 'That leads eventually outside and they could pick us up in an instant.' He moved closer and whispered in her ear, 'We need to go this way if we have any chance of getting ahead of them. We're lucky that they haven't already discovered the stairs on this end of the building, or they would have caught us by now.'

'Okay, that's all I needed to know,' Shelley said and shrugged her shoulders, then followed loyally.

Kevin gripped the metal bar and without making too much noise (except the odd grunt) wrenched it up with all his strength. Luck played a big part in his favour and he actually released the door. He expelled a great sigh of relief, easier than the last one he thought, recollecting the hatch in the sack pit. Kevin then pushed it open and tentatively slipped through. Shelley moved slickly behind him, and as soon as she entered the next section, she stood rigid and screwed up her face, putting her hands over her mouth.

'Whaa igg tha smwel,' her muffled voice filtered through her two cupped hands. Kevin peered round the doorway and grinned and gave out a chuckle.

'I can't understand what you're saying, move your hands from your mouth and maybe I'll understand better,' he said with a smirk.

'Yuk... what is that smell?' It was so bad it made her eyes water.

'Ah, it's nothing, you'll get used to it.' He closed the door behind them, not wanting to give any clues to the enemy as to their position. He then turned and continued through the darkened tunnel. The walls were thick concrete that concealed any noise from escaping

45

to the outside.

'It smells like a pig farm I visited once on a school trip.' Shelley squirmed, whilst frantically fishing in her pocket for a tissue to cover her nose and block out the odour.

'Oh, stop complaining,' he rolled his eyes up into his head and allowed himself a chuckle. Light was limited and the path in which they trod descended into a long slope. The air became colder and a cold wave of wind flooded the chamber. Shelley shuddered and rubbed her arms vigorously whilst still trying to mask the smell with the tissue. The walls were a filthy brown colour and reminded her of the connection between them and the smell that hung in the air. Pale grey slithers of light filtered through perforated manhole covers that were placed at various stages along the ground.

'It's not far now,' Kevin said, peering back at her, and a spark of excitement filled him. Bars of shade and light rolled over his face as he walked over the griddled cover plates.

'Brilliant, let's get out of here, then.' Shelley beamed and her eyes lit up, not wanting to spend anymore time in this place than she had to.

They came to a dead end and above them was another hatch door. It was only centimetres from the top of Kevin's head, so he reached up and touched it. It was a disc-shaped cover and had a long bolt that was pushed through an eyelet. It didn't take much to pull it back and release it, and then Kevin grasped the hand grips and lifted it free. What happened next was very painful. A gradual harsh shaft of white (like a torch beam) forced its way inside the gloom of the tunnel and

Shelley shielded her eyes from the glare. Kevin couldn't, because both his hands were taken up with holding the cover. He winced and painfully squinted, with both eyes watering under the pressure. Suddenly a continuing blast of welcome fresh air wafted over Shelley and Kevin's dirty faces. It forced the stench of the tunnel away, which gave them a chance to really breathe. Kevin gingerly protruded his head above the surface. He used the lid as a camouflaged helmet and scanned the area in a circular, three-hundred-and-sixty-degree rotation. It was all right, there were no Plogs in sight.

'I knew it, that's it,' Kevin exclaimed.

They climbed out and Kevin explained everything to her after replacing the lid.

'See that, that's the old sewage pit,' Kevin said excitedly and pointed out a vast area of brown bubbling sludge.

'No wonder it smells so bad. Yuk.' Shelley wretched again and slowly craned her neck. They were standing at the edge of a cliff face with a vast network of catwalks leading here and there, up and down, all over the plant.

'We were in the venting shaft,' he said confidently. 'See below us.' Kevin pointed to a large open pipe that protruded from the rock face.

'But we were originally inside a warehouse.' Shelley looked at Kevin in confusion.

'They shut the sewage plant down years ago and sealed it off, and used the connecting buildings for a warehouse,' he said. 'See that there?' He pointed to a large open-ended pipe. 'That's the old sewage pipe, it's been shut down for a long time, but it's been reopened and used for something else,' he explained. 'Plogs... they use the pipes to travel everywhere.'

'Why, why don't they walk on the surface like everyone else?' Shelley asked innocently.

'I don't know, but they only travel that way unless there are no pipes, and then they come above ground only for a limited time.' Kevin continued with his Plog lesson, 'The only exposed part is when they come out of that pipe and go along the walkway and enter the other pipe at the end. Look can you see it?' He pointed vigorously to the other side. 'That's where we have a chance to take the book and the device.'

'How do you know so much about this place, Kevin?' Shelley asked.

'My father used to run this place; he was in charge until...' He didn't say anymore and stared out into the bog.

'If you don't want to talk about things, Kevin, I understand,' Shelley said and left it at that. Kevin dismissed the rest of the conversation and concentrated on the job at hand.

'That's where we can do it, down there.' He pointed to a door just below where they were standing. There was a metal ladder with a handrail in front of them and it led to the walkway. They climbed down and stood on the cold flat metal surface. It felt unsteady and swayed slightly in the wind. They moved quickly along it and down the rusty steps. They were now on another long metal narrow platform. To their left was the open sewage pipe that Kevin predicted the Plogs were going to disembark from, and to their right was another open pipe where, Kevin surmised, they were going to disappear back into. They were standing in the middle, and the door Kevin talked about was dead centre in the distance between the two pipes.

'Darn it,' Kevin cursed.

'What's the matter?' Shelley said, interrupting his train of thought and chuckling at his use of words. She had never heard any boys say those words before.

'It's a chain,' he ranted angrily.

The door was a little taller than the both of them. It had a porthole two-thirds the way up, with a rather stained glass window set inside it. Halfway down the door and to one side, there was a hefty-looking lock. The padlock was quite old and was linked through a chain. This in turn looped through two eyelets that were fixed, one on the door, and one on the metal wall. Kevin gripped the lock tightly and turned it this way and that, and then he tugged it and prodded it and felt it as though it were a living thing. After a time he gritted his teeth and closed his eyes and shook his head vigorously.

'This is no good,' he said downheartedly, staring at the cursed lock in the palm of his hand. He stamped his foot in temper.

'Let me have a look?' Shelley urged him.

'It's too hard, Shell. We'll have to figure another way. We haven't time to mess about with it anymore, it could take hours to open and the Plogs could turn up at any moment,' he said scratching his head with his free hand.

'Let me have a look then, it can't do any harm can it?' she persisted as Kevin reluctantly moved to one side and let the metal lock fall. Shelley lent over and picked it up. It was heavy and took her two hands to lift. As Kevin had tried she did the same and wrestled with it for a few moments.

'Come on, Shell. This is useless,' Kevin complained impatiently. Shelley realised that it was an impossible task and also grew angry.

'All right, you win. This is useless,' she said, feeling defeated, and threw the padlock down. It banged against the two rusty eyelets and they were so weathered and aged from years of use that they simply broke off. The padlock fell to the floor, followed by the chain and a clanging sound that rang through the walkway. Kevin looked on in astonishment, but he wasn't as half as surprised as Shelley was. They peered into each others eyes and burst out laughing. It was good seeing Kevin laugh again, Shelley thought. He was so serious most of the time. For that brief moment his face lit up like a beacon and the torment was lost. The moment was brief, though, as Kevin's face turned quickly to the task ahead. He pulled the metal door open, and besides the elongated groan it made as it released, it also made Kevin smile.

'This is great,' he said with glee.

'Why?' Shelley asked in puzzlement.

'Can't you see it opens out and to the left and cuts off the passage way,' Kevin said looking very pleased with himself.

'So, when the Plogs come through we can stop them?' Shelley had thought it through first before saying anything.

'Yeah, but if we can push the door open when the

Plog comes past with the book and the device, we can block off the others before they have a chance to fight back.' He stopped in thought, then said, 'And if we're quick enough, we can get away, shut the door behind us, and lock the Plogs outside.'

Shelley stood in awe. 'Great plan, but what if it doesn't work out just as you say it will? What if the Plog with the device and book is in the middle?' she probed.

'Well, we'll have to wait and see,' he answered, feeling slightly annoyed at Shelley's negativity. With that, echoed footprints blasted from inside the giant sewage pipe. Both the teenagers were jolted into action.

'Come on, let's get inside,' Shelley urged. 'Kevin, how are you going to see where they are and which one to jump out to?' she half whispered.

'If I keep the door open slightly and at an angle, I may be able to see them coming, if I peek through this porthole,' He said it confidently and closed the door to a small gap. He peered through the slit in the door, and saw that they were indeed emerging from the opening. Shelley stood behind him.

'Great,' he said excitedly under his breath. 'The one with the book is in front of the others as well. Yes!'

Shelley could hear his heart beat clearly in the quiet of the little room. Hers was beating at the same pace. The metal walkway vibrated and rattled under the wave of foot steps. They were getting closer now, and Shelley saw beads of sweat running freely down the side of Kevin's brow and over his cheek. Kevin gripped the inner door handle with intense pressure, making his knuckles whiten. Shelley was beginning to find it harder and harder to breathe. She also began sweating and she clenched her hands into a fist. Kevin's breathing came in short, sharp bursts and he stepped back one step and slouched down below the sight line as the Plogs approached. Shelley's mouth opened and she held onto her last breath and instinctively eased back. She reversed a short step and gingerly touched her heel on a steel bar that rested against the wall, which fell and landed with an almighty clatter! Without a second to spare, Kevin pushed the door open and separated the small group of Plogs, leaving the desired one isolated. The creature didn't know what was going on and was stunned for a moment, which was all that Kevin needed. The force of the heavy door knocked all the Plogs behind it onto the floor. The teenager spun round, saw the book and gripped it, much to the dissatisfaction of the Plog holding it. He didn't let go and they struggled briefly. The book slipped out of both their hands and landed on the metal base. The brooch pattern that adorned the cover broke off and rolled. It stopped rolling and wedged itself in the pattern of the surface. Kevin had no time to grasp the two, and the book was too far away, so in the split second he had to think, he decided on one and picked up the brooch. The Plog grabbed the book and the other Plogs were already on their feet. Kevin leapt inside the doorway and gasped as he felt something grip his left shoulder. Shelley could see the Plog that Kevin had just grappled with pulling him back outside. She instinctively grabbed the door handle and pulled it shut. There was an almighty high-pitched screech, and Shelley saw the Plog's arm jammed in the door. She released the pressure and his hand withdrew as if sucked out. The bar that had fallen and given the game away was in her hand, and she threaded it through the handle, which acted as a latch. The door was now sealed, but the Plogs immediately pulled and wrenched it hard in a bid to get it back open. Shelley let go of the bar and stood staring at it. Kevin's voice brought her back to reality and she shook her head.

'Come on!' Kevin shouted, as he sped through the other door and along the corridor. Shelley broke into a sprint after him. There was a stairway to the upper levels of the warehouse, and Kevin bounded upwards, still grasping the brooch in his left hand. In the shadows of the building, Shelley did her best to keep up with him, but he was stronger and faster than her. She felt the coldness of the handrail as she pulled herself up the steps. Daylight seeped in the further she ascended and she could see Kevin plainly, until he quickly disappeared into the distance. At the top of the stairs was a long open corridor which led to another set of steps. Kevin was starting to climb them as she escaped the first set of stairs and made her way to the next set.

'Wait... wait for me, Kevin,' she called in Kevin's wake.

'Shell, keep up or we'll get caught.' Kevin's voice was mixed with the heavy thumping of their footsteps.

Deep in the bowels of the warehouse, the Plogs had rattled the door so much that the bar had slid off and released it. They were now quickly chasing the boy and girl and were filled with a deep anger at losing their prize.

First to burst through into the open air was Kevin, with Shelley only seconds behind. Kevin didn't stop; he just kept on running across the outer compound.

Shelley had made up some ground and was not far behind him. He made for woodland on the outskirts of the warehouse boundary fence.

'Kev... where are... you... going?' she said whilst trying to run and breathe and talk all at the same time.

'I don't know, just follow me,' he said as he pelted into the trees. Shelley continued on and ran through the treeline in pursuit.

Almost out of breath, she glanced back to see the warehouse. The Plogs still hadn't emerged from the old building. She turned toward Kevin and ran out of ground. She tumbled helplessly down a steep, grassy gradient. Panting for breath as she hit the bottom, she regained composure and sat up. She was dazed, and blinked her eyes for a moment or two. Once she had focused, she looked up the hill from where she had just fallen, and saw Kevin at the top. He was shouting something, but until she fully came to her senses she didn't know what he was saying.

'They're coming, come on, get up, they're not far behind,' he screamed and ran down the hill at full speed. He didn't stop and whistled past her. She got to her feet and turned to follow, then stood in awe.

Chapter 6

The Maze

About thirty feet in front of her stood a wall of tall trees, huge in stature. They were tightly knit, like a row of well-trained soldiers on parade. The line ran from right to left as far as she could see. There was, however, a small gap that looked invitingly like an entrance, albeit small, cold and dark. Kevin was still running, but he didn't run toward the hole, he ran along the outer side, missing the entrance completely!

'Kevin, where are you going? You're going the wrong way,' she protested and flung out her arms trying to draw him back.

'Come this way, Shell. We can get away down here,' he called back to her and enticed her to follow. He seemed really determined that she follow him.

'No, Kev, why don't we hide in there? We've got more chance of losing them in there. What's the problem?' she protested again sternly, still confused as to why he wasn't heading for the more obvious escape route.

'NO,' he answered defiantly, 'not in there.' And he stopped running and made his way back to her and grabbed her arm.

'Stop, Kevin, you're hurting, what's wrong?' Shelley winced, anxiously tugging her arm back.

'I'm sorry, I didn't mean to hurt you,' he confessed. He was anxious and looked deep into her eyes. His eyes were filled with a deep-seated fear, and Shelley could see the pain.

'No one ever comes out of there, Shell... it's... its evil,' he said in a lower, more sinister tone. 'One or two people have stepped in, just past the entrance and come back out again saying it's some kind of maze. They also said they heard things, terrible things in there, but the others who ventured further never came back. We can't go in there, Shell, we just can't.' There was tremble and finality in his voice, she looked at him and saw the ever increasing fear in his eyes.

'Where do we go, then? There is nowhere else,' she relented with a blank look, and with that last comment, as if on cue, the Plogs appeared on the brow of the hill.

'Well, it's too late now to go anywhere, look.' And when Shelley turned, she could see only too well the problem they faced. The blue creatures were scuttling down the slope and Shelley stood motionless staring back at them. She gestured toward the entrance of the forest, but Kevin gripped her arm again.

'No, Shell. You'll never come back.' Kevin looked anxious and scared at the same time. He peered into the bleakness of the entrance as he spoke. 'Once we're inside, we can't escape.'

'Kevin, look at the Plogs.' Shelley pointed curiously to the enemy. He turned to see and for once relaxed a little. They weren't moving any closer; in fact, they looked more scared than he did. One of them, Kevin could see, was holding the book, the same creature he had fought with to get the brooch. Kevin still felt the smooth warmth of the brooch in his pocket and it gave him a little more courage.

'They're afraid to follow us, they know the dangers,

too,' he said looking grim.

'We must go in, it's the only chance I have of ever getting back home. If they catch us now we've both had it,' Shelley said, her eyes were big and sad. Kevin eased off and let go of her arm and instead clasped his hand around hers. He knew deep down inside that he didn't really have a choice either. He turned and walked over to the opening.

They stood at the cusp of the maze and looked at each other. Shelley motioned with a nod and they walked further inside. Shelley glanced back once more to see the Plogs staring at her, but not making any attempt to follow. The teenagers walked a little timidly further into the unknown and stopped.

'Kev, have you got the remote?' He hesitated and shrugged his shoulders.

'There wasn't one, Shell, or not one I could see anyway, but I have the brooch,' he said positively. 'There may be a remote, Shell, but the Plog I fought didn't have it. In fact, looking at them out there, none of them seem to have it,' he concluded.

'You've got the brooch, but the most important thing... the thing I really needed you haven't got,' she paused. 'You said you would help me, Kev, but all you really wanted to do was get the brooch.' The look she held on her face was enough for Kevin to see how upset she was.

'No, Shell, I honestly tried to get the remote as well.' But Shelley wasn't listening to him anymore, she suddenly felt sick. Now how was she going to get home? Why did she have to follow those stupid Plog creatures in the first place? She could have been at home now, tucking into her tea and watching her favourite pro-grammes on satellite TV.

'Are you all right, Shell? You've gone pale,' Kevin asked guiltily, trying to re-establish his friendship with her.

'I don't see the point in going on, Kev,' she said downheartedly, 'I might as well give myself up to those creatures... I can't go home now can I?' She spun round and started walking back out. Kevin felt useless; he didn't know what to do.

'Shelley, stop please. There's one person I can ask about you and maybe she can help.'

But Shelley wasn't listening and continued to walk back toward the entrance, until she stopped dead! It wasn't there anymore!

'Wha-what's happened to the parting in the trees, it-it can't have disappeared?' she said in puzzlement. All she could make out now was an overbearing wall of green mesh. She craned her neck, but couldn't see over the top because the trees were as high as skyscrapers. Kevin darted alongside her and stood transfixed.

'This is impossible, this can't be,' he went on. They moved closer, and tried to create another hole. They pulled and clawed at the foliage, but it felt like woven steel. The weave of branches meshed together and made an impenetrable surface. Kevin clawed his way upwards in a bid to climb over, but it was also too brit-tle to climb and broke under his weight. He landed with a thud.

'What the devil's happening? This doesn't make any sense.' It was as if it was alive and had mended itself, like a finely crafted spider's web. Shelley eased back her head again and looked directly above at the gap in the treetops. Evening was beginning to form in the shape of cloud smothering the natural light and dimming the land.

'It's getting dark, Kevin,' Shelley said with a quiver in her voice.

'We can't stay in here overnight, there must be another way out.' Kevin stepped away from the hedge. 'There must be another way out.' He looked around and gestured to Shelley to go further in. The two made their way deeper into the forest holding one another's hand. They moved along a straight path and the ever-dimming light made it more difficult to see. Every so often, sounds emerged, a shuffle of leaves here, and a rustle of branches there. They eventually came to a three-way split, three identical channels tapering off in different directions.

'Great, what do we do now?' Shelley asked negatively.

'This is why they call it "The Maze",' Kevin said with a shudder. 'We should take one, any one.'

'I don't know... eeny, eeny, miny...' Shelley began reciting the old children's rhyme.

'Shell, what are you doing?' Kevin interrupted angrily. 'We haven't time for these stupid kids' games. It's getting darker by the minute and we have to get out of here,' he erupted.

'Fine,' Shelley said feeling miffed with his petty attitude, and gave him a look that could freeze porridge.

'Any way is good, this'll do,' he announced, and let go of her hand and bounded off taking the middle path.

She, on the other hand, was feeling hacked off at the fact he'd called her a kid. She stood her ground until Kevin had disappeared, and came up with her own decision.

'Well, I'm going this way,' she ranted, and stamped off in a different direction, muttering as she strolled along. Within a couple of minutes they both realised what they had done, and Kevin turned back immediately to find her, but he couldn't. Where was he now?

'Shell... Shelley, I'm over here.' Kevin's voice ripped through the empty corridors of the maze. Shelley heard him call to her, but couldn't quite make out where he was.

'Kevin... Kevin, where are you?' she called back with a tremble in her voice, 'I'm over here, Kev, please find me,' she pleaded. She was getting scared and turned back the way she had come, but the single path she had taken had changed from one road to a fork! 'Kevin... Kevin, please help me I'm lost.' The haunting voice of Shelley floated on the wind.

'Shelley, is that you? Stay there, I'm coming.' He picked up pace and made for the place that he thought he'd heard her calling from. 'Don't stop talking, Shell, or I'll lose you again.' Kevin moved along the winding corridors of the maze. It was almost dark and everything looked sinister. The branches of the trees looked like arms ready to grab anyone that came close. Strange noises seemed to seep through the forest as if the trees were talking to one another.

'I'm here, Kevin, help me... help me, please,' the pitiful sickly tone of Shelley called out invitingly. With a renewed determination Kevin followed the voice regardless of any danger.

Shelley, meanwhile, was getting into more of a muddle. *What is this maze all about? One minute you're going one way, the next another.* She came to another three-way split and puffed in annoyance. She raised and extended her right hand and pointed with her index finger to each entrance. She took the decision to go left this time and after only a few metres she came to a stop at a dead end. 'Aaargh,' she ranted and angrily stamped her feet on the ground.

'Shelley... Shelley, I'm over here, come on.' Kevin's voice sounded very close.

'Kevin, I'm here, keep talking and I'll find you.' His voice, though, was really difficult to pinpoint.

Darkness had swallowed up all that was left of the day. The only source of light was the moon's glow through a layer of thinning cloud.

'You're nearby, I can feel it, Kev.' She suddenly felt pains in her stomach from the anguish of fear, but she gathered all her wits and made her way to where Kevin was waiting.

'Help me, Shelley, help me.'

It seemed like Kevin's voice calling to her, but he didn't normally sound so weak and, for want of a better word, she thought, sissy! She ran along the darkened pathway and tripped over an outstretched vine, and ploughed headlong onto the ground and tensed her whole body.

'Kevin, help me please,' Shelley's voice called out pathetically.

'Don't worry, Shell, I'm almost there. I can hear you

and you're not far away now.' He came bursting through the undergrowth. He suddenly felt something grip his shirt tightly and tug him over to one side. It took him completely by surprise.

'Aaargh, gerroff me,' he ranted and suddenly felt his feet slide from under him and tip over a ledge. He landed on his backside and slumped onto his back. He looked up to see Shelley looking back at him with her hand still tightly gripped to his collar. His heart was pumping so hard he could barely breathe.

'What the... hell's... happening?' He waited for an answer. Shelley didn't say a word; she just eased her grip and pointed ahead. Kevin raised himself onto his elbows and gasped. The moon was high in the sky, and the clouds had all but disappeared. Its whitish glow poured down onto the sheer drop that lay before them. His eyes widened like dinner plates.

'That's why no one ever comes out of this maze, Kev, because no one ever survives the fall after the voice calls them to their deaths,' Shelley said. 'If I hadn't fallen over first, I would be down there now.' She pointed to the darkened depths below.

'What is this place? Let's get out of here.' He got up, and the two of them moved away from the area of danger.

'Where are you going? You must stay here, my children. You cannot leave.' The haunting tones of the ghost of the maze ranted thickly. The dense tree-soldiers began to close in and push the youngsters to their doom, like a slot machine in the amusements arcade, pushing the coins over the edge. Shelley's mouth dropped open like the drawbridge of a castle, and she felt goosebumps appearing on her arms and neck. Her teeth began to chatter, she shivered uncontrollably and also began to sob.

'This place is really alive, Shell,' Kevin gasped.

'I don't want to know, Kev; I just want to get out now,' she cried, totally terrified by the whole experience. Kevin could see a way out at one side of the maze. He quickly got up and stepped back on the ever-disappearing forest floor

'Run, Shell, run!' Kevin screamed, and caught hold of her hand, pulling her along behind him. As if on rollers, the trees moved slowly along the ground in perfect order, closing the gap of escape.

'Come on, Shell, we're nearly there!' Kevin screamed, and pulled her almost off her feet. The teenagers had only just made it, before the ghoulish tree-spirits had time to push them off the end. They briskly descended along the outer reaches and out of danger.

'Come back, come back, my children. You cannot escape.'

But they didn't stop. The children ran for all they were worth and didn't look back. They heard the sickening, screeching curses of the occupants of the maze ringing in their ears, damning them to Hell! They continued running, and took the pathway that led down a long, stony track and which would eventually lead to the 'mud flats'.

Chapter 7

Empty-handed

The creatures were in disarray as to what had happened to them. They were given a task to do, and as far as they were concerned, all was well. They'd gone back as they were ordered, and recovered the precious book that Scarrat had told them to collect. They puzzled it out and still could not believe that a bunch of children had stolen a part of the book, and that they had let it happen. There were squeaks and mumblings among them as they watched the trees swallow the two children up. There was a definite evil that waited in that maze, they could feel it. The aliens squabbled amongst themselves as to who should follow the children and retrieve the diamond. Not one of them would go inside, so they had no alternative but to face the consequences of Scarrat's wrath. They still had the book, though, but was that enough? One took the lead and ranted at the rest that it had to be enough. It was still daylight, and they were weary. Plogs disliked light and they would need to get under cover soon, but daylight was fading anyway, so it wasn't too bad. They turned away and scuttled along to the warehouse once again. They descended the stairs and made their way several floors down to where they had been ambushed. The small group continued their walk along the steel bridge until they came to the second entrance. They all felt more secure in their own environment. Once inside, they walked in so far, then the leader made the decision to rest a while. They slumped in their different places of sleep, and curled up just like a wild dog would.

Plogs only need complete rest for a short period of time, but when they woke up, the lead Plog screeched, in horror. The others were startled and turned to see what the commotion was all about, then immediately realised what had happened - the book was now gone too...

Slowly and hesitantly, the Plogs edged through the narrow corridor, trembling like jelly with every step. They knew the fate that awaited them at the end of the dim passageway. Behind the leader, the underlings held back a few paces, but continued on the relentless and unnerving walk through the gloom. Outside was cold, and there was now an angry wind that swept along the dirty alleys, back streets and shabby buildings of Scarrat Town. Inside, the Plogs edged ever closer to the overbearing, dark, wooden doors that were the entrance to Scarrat's headquarters. A feeling of guilt filled the very core of each one. Murmurings from behind gave the leader even more of a sense of foreboding. Up ahead he could see the familiar site that was always there to greet them. Guarding the entrance, and stood on each side of it, was a pair of mean Razzard Wolves, long overdue a meal or two. They reared up in intimidating fashion as the victims arrived. The wolves' eyes burned with a fire that penetrated the very hearts of the small blue people. Each wolf stood with its shoulders easily the height of an average Plog. The Razzards' hollow-sounding snarls shattered the silence and vibrated the Plogs' eardrums to the point of pain. Each wolf bared its needle-sharp teeth, which glistened with clear saliva and stretched downwards, hanging from each of their lower jaws. Razzard Wolves were dangerous, unpredictable and merciless creatures, and these were no different to any other of their kind. Abandoning its order to guard and stay put, one lurched forward in attack! The leader Plog shrank back and covered his face with his hands in a feeble attempt to protect himself.

'Ripper, get back... get back, you mangy brute!' the gravelly voice of the owner boomed from the now partially-opened doorway. 'Crusher, stay boy.' The other wolf did as it was told and remained locked in its position.

Ripper, already in mid-flight, quickly landed and slid to a stop within a few inches of his target. He turned and sheepishly headed back to his place.

The door opened fully and gave way to a figure much more evil than any wolf; his whole being wreaked of evil. He was tall, at least six feet, with broad shoulders. In the shaded hovel of the doorway, it was impossible to see his face. He wore a long hunter's overcoat, which flared out at the bottom and concealed most of the jackboots that he always wore.

'Come inside,' he goaded in a sickly tone, 'come, little ones, don't be afraid. I'm not going to harm you,' and he backed his way into the room, flexing his index finger in a bid to coax them in. Reluctantly, the group huddled together and braved their way past the hungry predators. Once inside, the Plogs were guided along a corridor and up a flight of stairs. The hunter glided through another corridor, then came to a stop at a huge wooden door. He opened it and walked inside to the centre of the room, then stopped in front of a large antique desk. He lent against the front of the desk and faced the terrified creatures. The room was furnished with a leather sofa to one side of the desk and a black leather-studded chair behind it. A dusty chandelier hung from a beautifully crafted ceiling with criss-crossed beams set into the plaster and elegant swirls cut deep into the wood. The beauty of the room didn't suit the shabby appearance of the man who stood in it. This man was the notorious Shadrack Scarrat, or 'The Hunter' as he was also called.

The bright light inside the room hurt their eyes for a moment, and they waited for their pupils to adjust from the darkness of the passageway. The light unfortunately also revealed the features of the tormentor's face. His skin was weathered, like a scarred cow-hide, showing years of turmoil. He opened his mouth to speak, and revealed two rows of brown, stained and chipped teeth. Dark patches underlined his menacing green eyes. He eased back and set his shovel-like hands to grip each side of the huge desk. He paused, then asked one deadly question, 'Where is the book?' His voice seemed to echo forever. The answer finally came, in the stuttered reply from the leader of the Plog group.

'It was stolen from us.' The lead Plog, like the rest of his people, had mastered the art of the English language and spoke it clearly, but when they spoke amongst themselves they used their own language. Shadrack's face changed from the sickly, caring person that had just invited them in. Now the real Shadrack Scarrat emerged - a cold and menacing being. His eyes narrowed, the channels in his forehead stretched and deepened, and his knuckles whitened from the weather-beaten brown skin as his grip tightened.

'Stolen from you by whom? Tell me,' he lashed back with distaste. His voice grew angrier, like the deep, gravelled growl of his pet wolves.

'There were two evil people, a boy and a girl, and they attacked us and took the book,' the leader said in his defence. He didn't mention the incident in the tunnel for fear of being ridiculed even further.

'A boy and girl? And you couldn't stop that from happening? Children overpowered the might of the Plogs?' the hunter queried in a ridiculing manner. 'Couldn't you keep up with the speed of the humans?' He gave a hearty laugh that cut the Plogs to the quick.

'They disappeared into the forest, just outside the warehouse. That place is evil, so they must be dead by now,' the small creature lashed back.

'Ah, the Maze. I know where they'll be by now, I can go around it and find their remains,' he said, in a velvet tone and a sneer. 'But you are useless to me now, can't even stop a couple of children. What good would you be to a real enemy?'

'Do not underestimate us, Scarrat,' the leader of the group fought back in defiance, welling up courage. 'We can still be a formidable force.'

'You failed me; I sent you on a journey, a journey I couldn't take,' he snarled at the Plog leader, 'I asked for a book and you couldn't even do that simple task.' He gave a look of utter disgust, turned away and reached across his desk. He gripped an ornament set at the side of the table and tilted it away from him. With his back to the petrified creatures, he gave himself a wry smile.

The Plogs waited for Shadrack to dismiss them with a warning, but that didn't happen. The wolf figurine clicked forward and released the trapdoor on which the Plogs were standing. They didn't have time to react and fell instantly! Waiting patiently below, and pacing back and forth in a figure of eight at the base, were the two hungry Razzard Wolves, Crusher and Ripper. As the trap door closed above them, the wolves licked their lips and widened their jaws for the influx of protein.

The last remnants of shrieks and screams emitted as the trapdoor automatically closed! Scarrat scurried around his desk with purpose and sat on his leather-bound chair. He paused for a moment in thought, then reached for one of the drawers at the front and pulled it open. Inside were scrolls depicting maps of the Reflections territory. He eagerly pulled out one he had in mind, rolled it out over the wide surface of his desk and weighted the ends with a couple of heavy ornaments that stood on a shelf behind him. Scarrat focused on a portion of the map, and ran his index finger over the smooth, leather parchment. He studied it for quite a while, and stopped. Thoughts of anger at the loss of the book and brooch washed through his mind. Why did things always seem to elude him? But this time nothing was going to stop him, he thought with defiance. He cleared his head and made a decision. Once he had put his mind to it, he rolled the map back up and placed it next to his shoulder bag. He moved over to the other side of the room, pulled out a key from a chain that was fixed to his hip and placed the key into a large cupboard with double doors. He gently clicked it and pulled the doors open. He stood proudly and gazed at his prized collection of rifles. Each one highly polished and kept in pristine condition. Scarrat chose the one he wanted from the set of eight, then pulled out a drawer beneath and picked up a box of cartridges. He closed and locked the cupboard and turned toward his rucksack. He left the room and returned after a short while. He filled the bag with food and drink, and hung a small lamp on a hook on the side. He also pushed his map inside and a compass. Some of the cartridges he placed in the loops of his belt, and the rest he put in an outer pocket, just in case he needed them urgently. He was all set.

'We have no time to waste; it's almost dark already and more difficult to track them,' he muttered to himself. He called his most trusted Plogs to go with him, then he whistled for his pet wolves. They entered the hall-way, a little heavy on the stomach after their filling meal.

'Come, you two, we have work to do,' he announced. The Plogs, the wolves and Scarrat went outside into the town and along the dusty road, down toward the woods. 'The longer their bodies are left, the more chance there is of somebody else getting the book.' He pressed on, with his troop of Plogs behind him, and his faithful mutts bounding on ahead, somewhat slower than normal with their heavy gullets. 'I want that book,' he snarled. He lit his small oil lamp and held it aloft. 'Come on, come on, time is precious. We'll go this way, it's quicker.'

Chapter 8

Monkey

'Stop shouting!' The voice cut sharply through the blackened cover of the trees. Katie held still, but her eyes flickered wildly around in her head.

'Hey, over here. Quickly, come on,' the voice hissed again. The schoolgirl slowly turned toward the forest and peered deep into the dense bushes, but couldn't make anyone out. A keen wind toyed with the ferns, and fanned the branches of the oak trees. Where was that voice coming from? she asked herself.

'Quickly, over here,' a now more prominent voice urgently called out. A sudden parting of branches and a dividing of the overgrown high grass soon revealed the perpetrator. There, standing two feet high, with grey fur and a perfectly round head, was... a monkey! And, unbelievably, a talking monkey at that! Katie was astounded!

It had a long tail, which curled above its head. As it got closer, she could make out its glassy black eyes and a dinky nose. Its long, slim arms extended from the primate's shoulders and connected with small baby-like, black hands. Its thin torso ran a smooth line down to its legs and two big feet, which looked out of proportion with the rest of its body.

'Quickly, they're coming,' the monkey persisted, beckoning urgently to her with a flick of his index finger.

No-no, this can't be happening, she thought, and shook her head, as if to erase a bad memory, but it was still there.

'You, you can talk?' she asked in a state of confusion.

'Of course I can talk. Haven't you seen a talking monkey before? Oh, I suppose you haven't,' he boomed back, sounding quite offended.

'No, I certainly have not,' Katie responded truthfully. She stood solid, unsure what to do.

'You're in danger, come and hide, please,' he pleaded. 'They're almost here, you're in grave danger,' the monkey repeated. Katie was torn between the urgency of the monkey, and whatever danger might be on its way, or indeed was he actually leading her into danger.

'What's coming?' she probed. 'Look, I have to go to that town and find help. I need to get home, and I'm hungry and thirsty. I don't know why I'm even talking to a monkey! I must be losing it, big time,' she conceded.

'Bad people, scary people. They'll hurt you if you don't come now,' he said, and began fidgeting in panic. He nervously darted his eyes in the direction she was heading and quickly scuttled back into the forest.

She was finally left alone again. Katie was still undecided, and waited a moment or two. Night had fallen and only the moon gave any form of light. The talking monkey seemed genuine enough, but he was talking, and that in itself was strange, but then again, everything in this place was weird. She finally gave in to curiosity and followed in the footsteps of the miniature ape. The forest was on an incline, and she scrambled up through the ferns and bushes and inside to the cover of the undergrowth. Soon, she was out of sight of the road.

'Where are you, monkey?' she called, and her voice seemed to stand tall in the denseness.

'Shssh, are you trying to get us both killed?' the monkey whispered from a particularly overgrown patch of fern beside her. 'Get down here, or you'll be seen for sure,' he urged.

Katie instantly dropped to her knees, and took in a mouthful of tall grass that stood proud from a cluster of stems. She spat them out immediately, screwed up her face and was about to say 'Yuk', when a small, black hand covered her mouth. She panicked and jerked her head back.

'Let me go...' she said, and wrestled with his arm, grabbing his wrist and pushed his hand away from her face.

'I'm sorry... I'm sorry. Shhh, please,' he pleaded, and his breath came in sharp bursts. She could hear the fear in his voice, and understood he was frightened. He then gently parted the fern branches, like you would a vertical window blind. They were overlooking the road, and the hidden pair had a good scouting position. They crouched down low for no more than a few seconds before the sound of panting animals came within earshot. Katie's stomach tightened and her breath changed to a pant, and realising this, the monkey slipped his hand on hers to soothe her.

The animals fast approaching were wolves; they had huge heads and muscled torsos, and moved purposefully and precisely, taking in all that surrounded them. Each one had yellow eyes like a demon's, and long snouts that lifted and sniffed at the winds.

It wasn't long before another figure came into the frame. The soft, yellow glow of a lamp raised high brought this person into view. The lamp unveiled a tall man in a long hunting overcoat and heavy looking jack boots. The top half of his face was hidden from prying eyes by the wide-brimmed hat that he wore. His mouth and chin were bathed in the yellow of the lamp, and the darkened crevasses of his skin showed him to be aged and weathered.

'Keep looking, boys, I need that book and the brooch,' he called out in a low gravelly voice. The monkey and Katie peered at one another in the blackness.

Following in his footsteps were a group of shaded creatures that were stranger to Katie than the talking monkey. These were small and difficult to discern in the shadows. They also moved along with purpose, but they were so far away that their faces were obscured. The two wolves continued their search, until one stopped and sniffed the air directly opposite the place where Katie and the monkey were hidden! The other wolf seemed to sense his companion's discovery.

'Crusher, Ripper... What can you smell, boys? Is it the girl and boy? They won't escape me,' the tall hunter barked with glee. Katie turned to the monkey and, simultaneously, the monkey turned to her. They could feel each other's warm breath, but that was all. She was about to speak and sucked in air, but he put his finger to her lips and whispered very lightly, 'Shhh...' His breath puffed over her face.

The two animals growled in low menacing tones and padded toward the place where Katie and the monkey were hiding. Katie tensed. They had nowhere to go, one move would give them away. She put both her hands over her mouth, her eyes were as wide as they could possibly go! She didn't breathe or move...

'I need that book, and the brooch that were stolen from these useless Plogs,' he rambled, whilst the alien group behind him gave a hidden look of disgust at his derogatory words.

Katie panted in quiet, shallow segments, whilst she dropped her right hand and gripped onto the monkey's hands with a tremendous pressure which brought tears to his eyes. He wanted to bawl out in pain, but obviously couldn't. The Razzard Wolves padded forward in hunt mode and sniffed intensely as they moved in, closer and closer, growling and baring their teeth with menacing ease. Katie almost screamed, as every muscle in her face tensed. The monkey's black eyes opened to their fullest and his mouth widened, showing a row of ferocious-looking pointed teeth.

'What have you found, you mangy mutts?' the hunter ranted impatiently from further back on the road.

Meanwhile, the blue creatures stood patiently and said nothing. The wolves were almost on them, and Katie was ready to stand and give herself up, but the monkey gripped her arm and she turned to him with fear in her eyes. The only sounds heard were the rustling of the undergrowth, the swish of the wind forcing its way through the trees, and the deathly growls of the two dog beasts. The lead wolf edged one more step, and out of the thicket right next to the hideout popped a nervous brown rabbit. It screeched and belted out from under the fern line like a bullet from a gun. Once past the dogs, it shot down the slope and out onto the road with the two surprised wolves instinctively in pursuit, knocking the hunter over in their endeavour.

'You stupid, useless, mangy brutes, don't waste my time with your fooling around,' the hunter exploded in a frenzy of abuse. He grappled on the ground for the lamp then stood up. 'Come back here, you fools,' he bellowed.

Katie and the monkey were as surprised as the wolves, but sat and kept quiet. The hunting party moved off, with the hunter still firing abuse at his sheepish-looking pets. Katie released her vice-like grip on the monkey and rolled onto her back. She blew out a long mouthful of air, and closed her eyes in relief. The monkey immediately cupped his hands and blew hot air from his mouth onto his palms. He then put his squashed hand under the opposing armpit, using his body warmth to ease the pain. He winced and flexed his fingers a few times to get the blood flowing again.

'That was really close,' the monkey gasped, still bringing life back to his limbs. 'They must be looking for you and your friend.'

'I came here on my own, but I was following my friend,' she confessed. 'Shelley disappeared, and the next thing I knew... I was here. As for the boy that the man mentioned, I have no idea.'

'We must leave now, just in case they come back this way,' the little monkey said with honesty.

'Who are they, anyway?' Katie asked, still feeling bizarre for talking with a two-foot high monkey.

'Let's get out of here, and I'll tell you on the way to somewhere safer.' The monkey led the way, deeper into the forest, and the girl walked by his side and listened intently to what he had to say. The moon gave light, but Katie stepped carefully.

'That man is evil; he rules this place and everyone in it. Anyone who challenges his authority doesn't normally live long,' the monkey conveyed with conviction. 'He is Shadrack Scarrat, and his father used to rule this land. Lord Fairbourne Scarrat ran Fairbourne Town with a steady hand, he was a good man.'

'Fairbourne Town, what part of England is that?' she questioned.

'England? I've never heard of that place. Scarrat Town is in our world of Reflections...' the monkey continued. 'This place is called Reflections, and the town Fairbourne Town, but when Shadrack returned from the wastelands he took over the town and re-named it after himself, and hence called the place where you were going... Scarrat Town,' the monkey said with a sniff, 'When Lord Fairbourne Scarrat was in charge, he held a brooch that gave him the power to rule the town and all the surrounding world of Reflections. But it was so powerful it drove him to the point of madness. Well, that's what people say, anyway. The stone is nestled in a crest made of precious metals, and the centre-piece itself is said to be steeped in powerful magic. Eventually, Lord Fairbourne could stand things no longer, so he took the diamond and headed to the outer-lands, but left his legacy to his deputy in a parchment and not to his son, Shadrack. Shadrack went raving mad, knowing he could not rule. He later headed for the outer-lands in search of his father, to steal back the brooch and return to rule Reflections.' The monkey hopped over a fallen tree branch and waited for Katie to follow. She climbed over in a more dignified manner and rejoined him.

'What happened then?' Katie asked, now deeply immersed in the story.

'Well, as far as I know, Shadrack never found his father, or the brooch. In between were quite a few years when Fairbourne Town was overseen by Deputy Craig Logan. He took to the authority that Lord Fairbourne had invested in him.

'But then came the Plogs. They came from nowhere, took over Reflections and killed all in authority that could not escape. Deputy Logan gave the parchment to his son, Kevin, before he was captured and killed. He told him to run away and hide. Kevin escaped, hid the parchment, and wasn't seen again.

'Then Shadrack Scarrat breezed into Fairbourne Town a little later with his two new pets, the fierce 'Devil Dogs', Crusher and Ripper, and immediately took control of the Plogs and renamed the place Scarrat Town. The Plogs were terrified of the savage dogs. Apparently, after one such Plog challenged Scarrat, his wolves tore the creature to pieces. They now have a real fear of Razzard Wolves, so Scarrat took his rightful place, as he saw it. The Plogs can travel to different worlds, and Scarrat sent them in pursuit of his father. They must have found a place in the outer-lands where Lord Fairbourne Scarrat used the brooch to cross the boundary of worlds. They must have the power to search the residue of time travellers and follow them. There is a place known to all through history as the 'Dawn of Reflections',' the monkey proudly announced.

"Dawn of Reflections', what's that?' Katie interrupted.

'It's a place where Reflections, this world, allegedly

opens up to other worlds, so the old legend goes, but no one has ever seen it happen. It also takes place at a certain time each year, or so the same legend says. The Plogs also must have found something else and brought it back - that book Scarrat mentioned. Scarrat must believe that there's a book that was written by his father. He must also believe that the brooch is the same one that he needs, too, listening to what he just said to his wolves.' Katie listened to all that was told to her with great interest.

'There is a book in the place that I have just come from, that had a diamond set in its cover. It must be that book.' She revealed.

'Wow, he only needs the book and brooch, then he can move through other worlds and take anything he wants,' the monkey said with bitterness. 'The way that Shadrack spoke earlier suggests that the Plogs must have found the book, and brooch, and relayed the message back to the other Plogs in this world, but obviously your friend and her new ally must have stolen them back,' the monkey surmised. Katie stopped suddenly and stared at her new-found friend.

'We've been talking non-stop and I don't even know your name, monkey,' she declared boldly.

'Tell me yours first?' he said cheekily.

'I'm Katie... Katie Hinge, now it's your turn,' she said and stood waiting for his answer.

'Why, Monkey of course, I'm not going to be a Gerald am I?' he retorted flippantly with a disconcerting stare, his beady black eyes glistening like freshly mined coal. Katie grinned to herself and put her hand over her mouth to stifle a giggle, not to appear impolite.

'Well, Katie, I know of a friend who might be able to help you to get back home,' Monkey said, 'Come on, follow me.' He paused for a moment to pick an insect from his fur that had been annoying him and proceeded to eat it, much to the disgust of Katie. He then quickly darted up a tree trunk and was soon lost in the network of branches.

'Monkey, what are you doing?' Katie called out.

'Don't worry. I'm only looking out to see if the way ahead is clear.' His echoed voice cascaded down through the forest foliage, 'I can't see much from this one, its too dark.' A little rustling of branches and leaves, and he was soon back on the ground again. A sparrow gently glided down and rested on a rather thick branch besides Katie's head.

'Hi, Mr Bird, how are you?' Katie asked politely looking at the bird and the bird peered back blankly. Monkey looked on and blew a deep sigh.

'Katie, what are you doing? Birds don't talk, everyone knows that,' he said shaking his head in disbelief and then turned to the serious business ahead. He scuttled up another rather tall but thin-looking tree and hung from one of the top branches. He stayed there a while and slipped almost quietly back down, only the gentle rustling of the leaves gave him away as he brushed past them.

'Everything seems all right as far as I can see, Katie. There are no lights in the forest, so Scarrat must be looking somewhere else.' Before Katie had a chance to ask anything, he was gone again and she tried her best to keep up.

'Where are we going?' she called from further back.

The monkey moved in swift, darting movements. He sped effortlessly through the forest, daintily sweeping along the long grass, then disappeared up another tree along its outstretched branches and over to another that held out its wooden limbs. He flew across at a fast, but smooth, pace and down again onto the ground below.

'Wait for me, won't you?' Katie cried in annoyance, trying her very best to keep up in the dim surroundings. The little monkey shook his head in dismay and went back to get her.

'Sorry, Katie. I keep thinking that you know this place as well as I. We haven't time to hang around, though, you know, so come on.' She stared at him in annoyance.

'Monkey, where are we going?' she asked.

'You'll see, now come along.' And off he went again.

'Wait, Monkey... wait for me, don't leave me again,' she shouted after him, suddenly realising that with Monkey's tree-climbing agility and speed, he could easily have left her to the mercy of those wolves and saved himself, but he chose to stay grounded and help her. She felt slightly guilty and thankful at the same time and was very relieved to see him come back towards her, slowing his pace.

'Oops. Sorry, Katie, but it's dangerous out here at night, we must move quickly,' he insisted.

'I know, Monkey, but I'm not a monkey like you, and I can't move as fast, so you'll have to stay with me. It's just too dark, and I'm scared and tired and hungry and thirsty and....' she complained.

'Do you always complain this much?' he asked as he interrupted her torrent of negativity.

'Yes, when I'm hungr...'

'All right, all right, I get the picture,' he replied, 'Good grief, it's not far now, anyway, Katie, honest.' So they continued on together hand in hand.

Chapter 9

The Mud Flats

The maze seemed like a distant memory as the two children came across the mud flats. The depth of darkness eased into a more manageable pre-dawn twilight. This in itself revealed the mud flats for what they really were. Flat, muddied ground obscured in a steamy grey mist, which spread for miles. All around the sounds of belching steam filled the otherwise quiet surroundings. The air smelt of scorched soil and decay and Shelley screwed up her face, repulsed at its toxic atmosphere. She was still feeling irritable after her ordeal in the maze; also tired, hungry and thirsty. Her feet hurt, she needed a shower and was in no mood for banter with anyone. So she walked forward without any thought.

'Stop!' Kevin shrieked in warning.

'Why, what's the matter now, Kev?' Shelley snapped back and whisked her head to face him.

'Don't move any further, step back two paces and follow me through this place,' he said commandingly.

'I'm not in the mood for your messing about, Kevin,' she said, ignoring his warning and she walked further on regardless. It took only a moment for Shelley to fall into the bog, oblivious to Kevin's continued protest. She plunged headlong into the murky, warm, smelly mud that quickly moulded itself to her shape and began pulling her down...

'Kevin, help...!'

'Don't struggle, don't struggle,' Kevin repeated frantically, but Shelley was already in full panic mode. Despite his shouts of advice from above she still tried to climb out on her own. The more she wriggled and thrashed, the more the mud enveloped and sucked at her frame and weight, draining her strength.

'Please hel...' she twisted and clawed at the soft mud to no effect.

Kevin felt helpless. He knelt at the bank, stretched out his arm and tried to reach and grab her, but she was too far in. Steam wafted in his face and stung his eyes. Luckily the mud in this particular part of the bog was only tepid, but he knew that further in, in certain areas, it was scolding hot. Shelley was comparatively safe for just the moment at least. He suddenly stopped panicking and concentrated his mind. He knew it wouldn't be long before the mud claimed her forever, so he had to come up with something fast. There was little, if nothing in the way of tools to help him. Light was still not strong enough to see far into the distance, so he had to leave her alone for a few moments.

'Kevin, where are you going? Don't leave me, please.'

With Shelley's screams still ringing in his ears, Kevin scrambled purposefully around the area looking for something, anything, that would help. Finally he spotted a darkened object on the ground and quickly made for it. It was misshaped and brownish like a sleeping animal. He had no time to be timid. So he grimaced and grabbed it with a certain degree of trepidation and, to his delight, found it to be a large sack. Kevin gave a wry smile and immediately dragged it over to the bog. It was heavy with moisture and awkward to manoeuvre, but he pulled with all his strength. Shelley was by now half-submerged. He was careful not to fall into the mire himself and could see that Shelley was on her side and still had her head, arm and leg free.

Kevin knelt on the ground beside her and very carefully heaved and spread the sacking out like a carpet to within centimetres of her body. He'd seen this done many years earlier and knew it would work.

'Shelley, climb up onto the sack,' he urged from the edge. 'Shelley, listen to me, grab the sacking and pull yourself on.' At first Shelley didn't seem to understand, as her face was slowly sinking into the mud. Her eyes were glassy and vacant.

'Shell, climb-onto-the-sack, come on,' Kevin called out once more in a slow, deliberate tone. He kept a solid grip on the other end of the material and waited. It must have registered, because she reached out with her one free hand and gripped it.

'That's it, now pull yourself up,' he repeated.

With the combined help of his motivation and the stability of the sacking, Shelley eventually crawled bit by bit up onto the matting. Once she was fully on, Kevin pulled as if in a tug of war against the Devil. He pulled and pulled and dug his heels into the soft soil and eventually dragged her out of danger. They both rolled over and collapsed into a sodden muddy heap and then eventually fell exhausted into a deep sleep.

They were spooked out of slumber by the hollow sound of animals howling. They sat up in disarray and Kevin recognised the unnerving whines of the Razzard Wolves right away. Neither Kevin nor Shelley could see past the mask of steam that slowly danced and billowed around them.

'It's Scarrat and his hounds, they've found us, Shell,' he whispered. It was full daylight, but the mud flats were always in a state of camouflage, which was fully to their advantage.

'What are we going to do, Kev?' Shelley trembled with every word.

'At the moment, they can't see us and we can't see them, but those wolves will smell our scent and it's only a matter of time before they catch us,' Kevin responded dismally. The hunting party were getting closer by the minute and Scarrat's rasping voice was heard above all the commotion.

'Where are they, boys? Go find them for me, eh?' This made the animals' movements more intense and the pitch of their hunting cries increased.

'Follow me, Shell,' Kevin whispered as he got up and made his way through the treacherous bubbling pools. Shelley, a little more cautiously, followed after him. She manoeuvred through the dense, cloudy atmosphere, almost losing sight of her leader.

'Kevin, slow down,' she pleaded in as low a shout as she could manage. She lost sight of him and panicked and stopped. Behind, the snarling beasts were almost on her and tears formed on her tormented face. Something gripped her arm and she flinched and let out a short scream, her eyes flashed wide open.

'Come on, we've run out of time,' Kevin persisted. Shelley let herself be pulled along, dragged more than anything else... until he stopped. A screeching howl rasped through the mud flats like a saw through metal.

Kevin plunged into a mud pool and Shelley felt her arm being tugged downwards.

'Jump in, Shell, quickly.' Kevin desperately pulled at her arm.

'I can't, Kevin, I really can't.' Shelley shivered at the thought.

'You must, Shell. It's safe, trust me, or I wouldn't be in here.' He gently pulled her arm once more, 'Please,' he whispered. She gathered all her courage, closed her eyes and stepped in. The warm mud squelched under her weight and caressed her body like a giant hug. But it wasn't a weighted, sucking mud that had trapped her like last time, it was more a soothing, warm feeling... until the smell hit her and she heaved. Shelley could feel the bottom under her feet and felt more relaxed. Kevin held his finger to his lips signalling to her the need for quiet, as he guided her under the bank. She had to wade along and dip down under the gap in the surface, which brought the mud to just beneath her chin. They cowered motionless... waiting to be found out.

Scarrat's wolves were growling at a low pitch hastily searching, only centimetres above their hideout. The vicious brutes dipped their heads down to the mud surface and sniffed frantically. Kevin and Shelley could see the underside of both their jaws literally within touching distance. The mud plopped and steamed at low temperature and a big bubble popped and splashed over one of the wolves' snouts. He yelped in annoyance, shook his head rigorously and pulled back, also spooking the other. Razzards hate water and bathing, especially in mud, didn't really appeal to their nature. The teenagers held their breath and cringed.

'What have you found, boys?' The devilish voice of Shadrack Scarrat boomed overhead. 'Nothing, you've found nothing, and we almost had them,' he ranted. 'You mangy flee-bitten, useless wolves,' he scolded. 'Come on, let's go further along, they must be here somewhere. They weren't at the bottom of the cliff, so they must still be alive. How they got out of that creepy maze I don't know, but they won't evade me much longer,' he said and his voice faded into the distance.

'I think he's gone, let's get out of here,' Kevin said, still whispering and trying not to let his jaw drop any lower than the mud line. Shelley just nodded; she felt sick and wanted to leave more than anything else in the world. But when they tried to move forward they found they couldn't! They weren't stuck as such, but the soft mud underfoot was disintegrating with every movement. Shelley and Kevin found themselves slipping backwards. They grabbed the ceiling of warm clay above, but it came away in handfuls and their bodies suddenly disappeared under the murky surface and down into the gloom. Shelley struggled to hold her breath in the dark brown mass. There were no footholds or any kind of grip. The pair twisted around like clothes in a wash cycle, waiting for their impending deaths. Everything was happening so fast, and several times they felt the other's body make contact. They tried to hold onto one another during these brief episodes, but couldn't.

For a moment, they were out of the mud tunnel and flying through the air. It was still pitch black, but they could feel the blast of wind across their faces, and each took huge gulps of air, coughing and choking in the process. Shelley tried to scream, but nothing came out.

They were falling further and further, until they splashed down into another pool of liquid. Were they falling down a sort of mud waterfall or fast-moving river? It didn't feel as thick as the mud this time; it felt more like a warm river. It was still too slippery to stop the forward motion, so on they went. As if in a non-stop fairground ride, they flew through underground tunnels, but the watery fluid was shallower and they could breathe. The fast-paced stream sloshed at the sides, and echoed down through the cavernous tunnels. The course of running fluid dipped and twisted, not giving them time to work out an escape method. At the last point in their journey it sucked them down into a whirlpool and catapulted them up into another vast expanse of water. They were forced up through the surface. Their coughing and screeching resounded off the walls making it sound as though there were more people than there actually were. There was also some light illuminating the cavern, so they could see the bank and made for it.

The pair sat on a rock for a while not talking. Shelly breathed heavily until she could take shallower breaths and she felt calmer. Kevin sat quietly next to her pondering, and they looked around. The light came from a crack in the ceiling of the cave and shafts of pure, luminous white revealed the scene. Shelley noticed the water was clear and blue, the same as the sea in Spain. She also saw that their clothes were mud-free, and the lake had cleaned the rest of them, too! Even though they were in a cave, it wasn't cold at all; in fact it was quite warm. Peering further to the centre of the lake they noticed that the water of the lagoon bubbled and steamed like the mud of the mud flats. The simmering surface water was interrupted to one side of the cave by a large waterfall. Slow-flowing, white water spewed over the rocks and splashed gently into the lake. Shelley assumed the waterfall was ice cold, because when the cold temperature of the waterfall hit the warm water of the lake, clouds of steam lifted into dancing shapes. The thinning vapour created a colourful rainbow which made the whole scene look magical. She felt a thirst, which was especially strange as she'd just been through a water-filled nightmare. She got up and waded around the edge of the lake to the running water. Kevin followed on behind. She reached out and cupped her hands and filled it to overflowing. In turn they sucked in the water from their dished palms, but the delicious taste soon chilled them into brain freeze.

'You all right, Shell?' Kevin asked and touched her shoulder.

'Yeah, I'm fine, a little shaken, but fine,' she said smiling a deep long smile, 'Sorry I didn't listen to you, Kev. It was stupid of me to carry on walking when you told me to stop.' She paused and said, 'You saved my life again.' Kevin didn't know what to say at first and paused.

'As long as you're okay, that's the main thing,' he confirmed awkwardly.

'It feels good to be mud free,' Shelley said mockingly, 'You do take girls to the smelliest places for a date.' Then she looked hard at him and burst out laughing because his face was as red as a beetroot. Kevin stood there a little confused at the teasing he was getting. The whooshing of the waterfall made him remember the journey that brought them there and that made him remember the brooch. His facial expression suddenly changed from embarrassment to panic.

'What is it, Kev?' Shelley asked not knowing why he had changed. Kevin thrust his hand into his pocket and poked around inside until he felt the brooch and took it out and turned away from his friend. He breathed a sigh of relief and caressed it in his palm. The metal was warm and rigid and the diamond in the centre sparkled. He toyed with it for a while and was going to replace it back in his pocket.

'Can I take a look at it?' Shelley said peering over his shoulder, slightly annoyed at the idea of being left out. At first Kevin was reluctant to show her. It was his and only his to keep, but he relented and slowly handed it to her. She held it out in front of her and stared at its beauty almost hypnotically. Its twisted golden outer crest complemented the myriad of colours that flowed from the diamond in the centre.

'It's amazing, Kev. I've never seen anything like it before,' she said bursting with excitement.

'It's also very deadly if put in the hands of someone evil.' He reached out and Shelley handed it back. Kevin slipped it back into his pocket. Shelley looked at him with a tinge of fear, fear of what might happen if Scarrat ever got hold of it.

'Shelley, we have to get out of here.' Suddenly, there was a grumbling sound coming from Shelley's stomach and, as if feeling left out, Kevin's stomach began to rumble in unison.

'I'm starving, Kev; we're going to die aren't we?' she gushed holding her rather painful belly.

'Of course we're not, we've just got to find something to eat, come on,' he said as he began walking toward a chink of light that caught his eye in the far end of the cave. Shelley quickly sped up behind him and saw the same. She felt a little more comfortable as he led the way, because his manner was always so positive; it made her feel stronger in herself. He was right because the closer they got, the bigger the pure beam became. Soon they were outside in the cool air, but it was early morning and not yet fully light. Kevin laughed out loud.

'What is it, Kevin?' Shelley asked curiously.

'It's this place, I recognise it. Wow, I recognise it, great,' he shouted gleefully.

'Where are we, then?' Shelley said smiling.

'We're not far from where we need to be, and I think I can find us some food.' His face was filled with joy. 'There should be a small shack across the way there, where the fishermen used to go to stay on their fishing trips. Down in the valley is a lake everyone used before things went bad,' he said with bitterness in his voice.

'So we have to fish for our food?' she continued dismally.

'No, you nutter,' he laughed, 'They used to keep supplies in that shack, you know, tins of stuff.'

'I hope there's a tin opener, then, because the way our luck is running we'll have to bite our way through the tins.' Shelley grinned and off they headed in the direction of the shack. Surely enough where Kevin had said the fisherman's shack would be, there it was. It didn't look much to Shelley; it was literally the size of a large garden shed. It had a sloping roof, a window and a door; there was also a porch with an upright timber at each end.

'That's it, Kev?' she uttered sceptically.

'Don't knock it, Shell. If we find food in there then maybe you won't be so negative,' he said sharply, annoyed at her scepticism. Kevin walked up to the door and saw that there was a small padlock securing it. He scoured the ground outside and found a medium-sized rock. Without much retaliation, the lock gave way and broke off. Kevin pushed open the door and suspiciously ran his eyes over the inside before entering, even though it had been locked anyway.

'It's fine, Shell, come on,' he said and gestured with a wave of his hand. It was dim inside, but not to the point of pitch. It smelled of old fish and Shelley pegged her nose with her fingers.

'Oh, it reeks in here, Kev.' She winced.

'What did you expect, Shell? A perfume stall?' He grinned. There were cupboards on one end of the shack and with hope in her heart, Shelley opened them up to find a few tins of beans and rice pudding, and also a tin of corned beef and a tin opener.

'Wow. Great!' Kevin cheered. There was also a pot, but no stove and on further investigation a box of matches.

'How are we going to cook this stuff?' Shelley asked disappointedly.

'Good grief, Shell, haven't you cooked on a campfire before?' She looked sheepishly back at him. 'You haven't, have you?' She shook her head. 'But you're a girl; all girls can cook, can't they?' She shook her head once again. Kevin stared back at her in total amazement. He had a fire going in no time and cooked everything in the pot, letting it cook slowly. They both ate until they were full. Afterwards they rested for a while and later they were ready for the task ahead.

'Are you ready for this?' He almost whispered and Shelley nodded. So off they went on the journey into the void.

Chapter 10

Home

Katie continued following the talking monkey as he led her through the ever-threatening forest. All around were the sounds of strange hoots and shrieks, of snarls and rumblings in the long grass. Katie shivered at the thought of the origin of the animals emitting them. And above, high up in the overhanging foliage, there were hovering branches that seemed to reach out as if the trees were living demons. The footpath and dipped into a channel at the foot of a giant tree stump. Its monkey carried on towards his destination with a determined pace. Eventually they descended along a jagged twisted root had five curved knotted limbs that clawed the earth like a giant hand.

'Where are we going, Monkey?' she pestered time and time again.

'Keep going, come on. Not far now,' he said, and slowed down. The words 'Not far now' were strung out over miles and miles of countryside, and didn't mean anything at all to Katie after a while. The words, 'Where is he taking me? I can't go on much further,' rolled round inside her head.

'Katie, step over here and we're there!' he said with a renewed excitement and Katie sighed thankfully.

A full moon bathed the land with a luminous light and cast shade in pockets of the landscape. In the last half-mile or so Katie noticed it had been an uphill climb. The ground was slippery, as the damp evening mist moistened the grass and wet her trousers to the knee. Katie was tired from the whole surreal experience, her entry into this new world. Then there was the monkey that actually spoke to her, also the hunter and his two ferocious wolves, and the blue creatures mixed with the exhausting trek across the wilderness. It was all too much and she sat down and burst into tears. Monkey heard her sobbing and doubled back. He stood over her and saw the glistening tears that reflected in the moon's glow.

'What's the matter, Katie?' he said in a soft and soothing voice.
'I-I just wanna go home,' she blubbed. Monkey sat beside her and put his arm around her shoulder.

'Come on now, give me time and I'll get you home. I promise,' he assured her confidently, and gently squeezed the curve of her shoulder with his cupped hand.

'How did I ever get into this mess in the first place?' she sobbed uncontrollably.

'Helping your best friend is the answer to that, I think.' The little monkey seemed to brim with charm and intelligence and a deep understanding of human feelings. This made Katie feel a lot better, just listening to his words of wisdom and encouragement.

'Come on, miss.' He tugged at her arm and she rose to her feet. 'Let's get you inside and get a nice hot drink and some food inside you.'

'Get me inside. Are we here, then?

'Why, yes,' he replied.

'Thank you, Monkey,' Katie responded and her heart jumped at the thought of a hot meal and drink;

she was starving.

'Where is it?' she asked with a hint of desperation.

'It's here. Look. Can you see it?' Monkey raised an arm into the darkness and pointed the way. The ominous dull glow from the night sky revealed a large barn-type building, only metres from where they had stopped. Were it not for Monkey, Katie would never have seen it. It didn't matter, though; it was shelter from the cold night air. It may also be safer inside that, than being exposed to the forest, she thought.

'Come on, let's get inside,' she announced with renewed vigour.

The ground rose at a steep angle and pulled at Katie's calf muscles. She got to the entrance and almost couldn't go any further. Monkey led her inside the building by pulling the large wooden door open a fraction, only enough for them to squeeze through. It was blindingly black inside and there was a heavy musky smell that filled the air, like decaying wood and metal. It smelt familiar somehow and Katie searched her memory for an answer. The monkey slipped into the shadows and Katie could hear him fumbling around.

'Where are you, Monkey?' she called out and groped around trying to get some bearings as to where she was, but it was hopeless. She didn't want to hurt herself so she stood still. There was a tinkling and a sharp scoring sound and then Katie understood as the monkey lit the wick with the flame of a match. It glowed pale blue at first and then gradually burned to a full deep yellow feather. Monkey replaced the glass flute and the oil lamp lit every corner.

Suddenly the mystery of the strange odours that stirred old memories within her came flooding back. A huge smile opened up her tired face and filled her heart with glee. The barn was the home to a railway carriage.

'Wow, this is great.' Her sullen mood was forgotten about in a moment, and even the thought of food and drink were lost in her excitement. The body of the wagon was wooden and very old, and it was also fire-engine red, Katie's favourite colour. The paint was badly flaking in places and the wheels were rusted from years of neglect. It had three windows each side, which were mostly broken, and a door at one end with a handrail and steps to climb on board. It was in disrepair, but it didn't dampen her enthusiasm. Katie couldn't understand why the trailer was on sloping ground. The whole carriage was held fast with two huge wooden wedges.

'You like my home?' Monkey asked with his best monkey smile.

'Yes, I love your home,' she beamed.

'I take it you like trains?' the little monkey asked curiously.

'Well, my father loves trains, and he used to take me to watch them pulling in and out of the station when I was younger,' Katie explained.

'Well, welcome aboard,' Monkey said, stepping up the metal steps and onto the wooden platform. Katie gripped the handrail and boarded the old carriage. It was a rear section trailer and Katie stopped for a moment before entering, to reflect on the journeys it must have made.

'Come inside, Katie, and take a seat,' Monkey insisted. Inside, though, was nothing like she imagined it would be. All the original furniture had been removed and replaced with a makeshift table and chairs. There was a bunk bed on one side and some old carpet matting covering the wooden floorboards. Over in the corner where monkey was now situated was a cooker with a tubular chimney which elevated up through the ceiling. There was also a small moth-eaten settee next to the table. Katie walked in, and sat on one of the chairs at the table.

'How did you find this place?' she asked. Monkey busied himself with lighting the stove and placing a kettle on the flame.

'I think this carriage was coming to the end of its life,' he said as he placed a cooking pot next to the kettle on the stove, 'The interior had been stripped bare and it was left here, I think to be scrapped. The railway line was closed soon afterwards to make way for a new line through Reflections. The workmen used this carriage to sleep in and have breaks, and so they put all this stuff inside. I found this place after the workers had left. There's a store room at the back, with tins of food and dried milk and tea, enough for me to live here in hiding without Scarrat finding me, otherwise he would have killed me by now. He never ventures this far into the forest, anyway, so it stays hidden,' he said with relish.

'How come you can talk, then?' she probed. The monkey could see by the determination in her eyes that she wasn't going to be fobbed off without an answer.

'I was Lord Fairbourne Scarrat's pet monkey. I could do things the other pets couldn't do. I could not only do the normal tricks, but I could also make a cup of tea and I was trained to do what humans do, as this amused Lord Scarrat,' he said as the light from the lamp reflected in his round beady eyes. 'I had noticed this wonderful brooch set in gold that my Lord wore and when he was asleep one night I went into his chamber. The diamond that sparkled at the centre looked so pretty I just wanted to touch it. One thing that I'd always wanted to do and wished everyday that I could, was talk and understand humans. When I touched the stone, all of a sudden it happened. I didn't show anyone, and not long after this took place, the brooch was gone and so was my Lord. Soon after that Shadrack went, too. And then the Plogs arrived. I escaped before I was captured, and that was when I found this place.'

'But why does this Shadrack Scarrat want you dead?' Katie asked seriously.

'Because he wants to kill anything that made his father happy, and I was his favourite pet.'

With that confession the kettle began steaming, and Monkey produced two cups and continued to pour out tea from a small teapot. The small pot that he had placed on the stove earlier was bubbling away with a wonderful aroma of stewed meat and vegetables. Katie felt her stomach rumble. She breathed in deeply and closed her eyes; the delicious smell was actually toying with her taste buds and her mouth began to water. Monkey produced a dish and ladled a generous portion of stew into it on the table in front of Katie. He also poured out a mug of steaming tea.

After she had gorged herself on stew and drank the tea, Katie sat on the soft mattress of the bottom bunk and sank back into the soft pillows. It wasn't long before her full belly and the fatigue of the journey took its toll, and she fell into a long, deep sleep.

She woke suddenly with the sensation of movement. She blinked her eyes and tried to make sense of where she was, but it was too dark. There it was again, a jerking motion throughout the room. Katie then realised where she actually was... in the railway carriage where Monkey had brought her. She sat up sharply and hit her head directly on something hard.

'Ouch!' she squealed in sheer agony and rubbed her forehead vigorously. She felt around and understood that she was on the bottom bunk of the bed. The sharp shuddering movement gradually increased and a thud, thud, thudding sound came from the same direction and shook the whole compartment.

'Ome on... ome on.' The muffled sound came from outside.

'Monkey, Monkey, is that you?' The thudding stopped as quickly as it started and the trailer began to move in a slow forward motion. Katie was scared and was about to call out again when a small figure entered through the door, panting and fighting for air.

'Katie, hold onto something... anything,' Monkey gasped.

'Wha-what, I-I don't understand,' she responded vaguely in a stutter.

'Just hold on quickly, there isn't time.' This time Monkey was almost screaming, so Katie did what she was told and gripped the first solid object that she could feel. The wagon picked up speed and Monkey shouted in a high-pitched squeal... 'BRACE YOURSELF!'

There was a second or so of nothing, and then the truck burst through the barn doors and out onto the old railway track. Katie was propelled forward and tumbled to the ground, but she didn't let go of the handrail. Monkey was already gripping the metal handle of the back of the door. The moment of impact, though, dislodged the cooker and it was shunting straight towards him. He immediately scampered up the side of the wall and clung onto the overhanging luggage rack. The cooker slammed into the back of the door just where Monkey had been standing, and knocked it off its hinges and out onto the ground.

'What's happening, Monkey?' Katie rumbled, her voice vibrating with the continual shuddering of the runaway train carriage. The noise of the wind rushed in through the open compartment, making it almost impossible to hear anything.

'The Plogs, Katie, the Plogs have found us, and our only escape was by moving this carriage,' he shouted from the top of the luggage rack, the rocking cabin almost shaking him off.

'Where are they now?' she bellowed back, and with that, to her and the monkey's dismay, they saw a small dark figure climbing up into the compartment over the cooker that blocked its way. The breaking dawn behind silhouetted its oncoming charge.

'Monkey, they're coming!' Katie screamed. She quickly groped around, furiously trying to find something to defend herself with. Her eyes burst into life when she felt a metal handle. The Plog was halfway along the cooker top and was crawling like a baby to get inside. Without a moment's hesitation, and with Monkey looking on helplessly, she aimed and tossed the instrument into the intruder's path. It flew through the air and caught the creature square in the face. His look of surprise was priceless, as he, and the saucepan, were propelled out through the open doorway. He tumbled into a nearby field and straight into a sewage pond.

'Are there anymore?' she shrieked, but with a certain cocky smirk.

'Well done, Katie,' Monkey said smiling proudly, 'I think that's the only one,' he assured her, but kept a close eye just in case. There was a sigh from both of them, but it was short lived... The carriage was picking up momentum the further it descended the long winding slope. The compartment rattled and creaked with every canter and jolt.

'Monkey, we have to get out of here,' Katie babbled, whilst getting back up onto her feet.

'It's going far too fast to jump off, and there isn't a brake to stop us either,' Monkey cried as he climbed down from the luggage rack. They met in the middle. Trees and bushes rushed past the windows of the speeding carriage, as if diving out of the way.

'It'll probably be all right, Katie, it'll slow down eventually and come to a nice easy stop somewhere,' he said calmly with an air of confidence. Daylight was flickering through the open windows, and a huge bar of white light gradually bleached the space where the door had been. 'Yes, that's right, it will stop on its own,' Monkey continued with a smile.

'Well it had better stop before too long,' Katie retorted, raising her voice to a near screaming pitch.

'Why, Katie? Just enjoy the ride like me.' Monkey

was staring out of one of the side windows, taking in the view like a tourist.

'Because there's a dead end up ahead!' she shrieked, pointing ominously toward the doorway. Monkey turned and saw Katie staring urgently further down the line where there was a partition blocking the track.

'Oh dear!' Monkey peered into the distance with a twang of doubt in his quivering voice.

'What are we gonna do, Monkey?' she whispered at first, then belted out, 'WHAT ARE WE GONNA DO, MONKEY?' Katie then grabbed the monkey's shoulders and shook him until he could almost see double.

'K-A-T-I-E, g-e-t a g-r-i-p.' He recoiled and broke away from her manic embrace. Monkey darted all over the compartment looking for a means of escape. He stopped suddenly and turned to Katie with a look of despair in his eyes.

'We have to jump...' He didn't blink; he just continued to stare at her.

'Are you nuts?... I-I can't,' she stammered. 'Monkey, I really can't do this.' Her eyes were wide and her mouth fully open as she shook her head.

'Katie, we must... NOW!' he screamed impatiently.

Katie's heart felt as though it was trying to escape through her throat. The only time she had felt this scared was when she had followed her friends onto a roller-coaster ride. This, though, had no bars holding her in and the ride was for real. Very real!

'Look, Katie, we either jump, or we crash.' He shrugged his shoulders, and gave her a look of pure desperation.

Katie stood motionless and looked away from the oncoming danger. The wind hissed violently in her ears, and the only other sound was the clumpity-clump of the railway track. She tried desperately not to look ahead, but her curiosity got the better of her and it pulled her eyes toward the danger as if by a magnet. Her eyes opened to the widest they'd ever been and her mouth resembled a pocket on a snooker table. 'Okay, okay, let's do it now quickly, so I haven't anymore time to think about it.'

Katie and Monkey took a large gulp of air and held hands. He stepped closer to the edge and had to tug at Katie to do the same. She looked down at the ground rushing by and it made her feel sick. She couldn't breathe, her chest seemed to retract and cut off the oxygen to her lungs.

'Now, Katie, come on.' The monkey leapt forward and pulled Katie with him. She tried to resist and held back through sheer terror, but it was too late. She had already overbalanced and gone past the point of no return. The two of them dropped out of sight. A few moments later there was a tremendous crash as the speeding carriage went hurtling head-on into the wooden blockade and shattered into a million pieces. The explosion could be heard for miles around. Suddenly the sky was filled with floating wooden splinters and wheels and glass. The sound eventually tapered off into the distance and moments later... emptiness. It was as if nothing had happened. All that remained were the last of the floating timbers and a dusty haze that hung in the air, which was whipped away by the north wind.

Chapter 11

Voice from the Void

The sun was high in the sky in the world of Reflections as they entered the rock ledge that overhung the void. But its light couldn't penetrate the depth of the ravine. The ledge itself was shaped like a giant tongue, flexed ready for dinner. The fissure was as wide as it was deep. Shelley gripped Kevin's arm and gingerly wavered at the edge. Kevin leant forward to peer into the gloom and he too became nauseous. Shelley stared ominously over the rock lip, and as hard as she tried, could not penetrate the chasm of blackness. A cold, cutting wind came from behind and nudged them closer to the tip. Startled, they both tensed and stepped back.

'What is this place, Kev?' Shelley whispered into his ear and held on tightly to his hand.

'It's a place for answers, and maybe a way to get you home.' He began searching around on the ground for something.

'What are you doing now?' she asked, following his movements.

'You are not going to believe what I'm about to tell you, but listen anyway,' he explained, 'Ah, here's one.' He picked up a rock and weighed it up in his hand. 'This will do,' he said, appearing pleased with himself.

'What?' Shelley stood baffled by his antics, and stood with a blank look on her face.

'Wait a moment and let me explain, Shell. You're way too inquisitive,' he said with relish at being in control for once. 'She is the voice of the void,' he put his fingers to his lips signalling her to stop interrupting, as she was bursting with questions. 'And when I drop this rock down into that hole, She will come alive.'

Shelley felt a shiver rack her whole body at the mention of coming alive. She couldn't hold out any longer.

'What is She? Who is She? What are you talking about?' Shelley burst into a frenzy of questions.

'I don't know, nobody does,' he relented, 'But She knows things, and only Lords and Royals are allowed to visit and ask, otherwise she won't answer. But things are different now. My father was given the rule of the land after Lord Scarrat disappeared, so as his son, I'm the only person left. I hope She will speak to me.'

Kevin moved closer to the edge, and reaching out his arm he released his grip on the stone. It slipped away silently and soon vanished in the gloom of the pit. They waited with ears strained. A keen wind swirled and whistled its way beneath them, until there were a few echoed cracks as the rock hit the bottom. A heavy silence filled the void. There was nothing. Kevin and Shelley looked at each other and Shelley gave a gesture of 'What was that all about?'. But then it happened. Deep in the bowels of the mountain there came a penetrating growl at first and then a throaty shriek.

'WHO DARES DISTURB ME?' The chorus of tongues shook the ground underfoot and reverberated up through their spines.

'I-I am Kevin of Reflections... And I would like your help?' he stuttered.

'I have no desire to help anyone, do not disturb me

again,' the voice reacted and faded away. Kevin stood motionless, not knowing quite what to do. Shelley flashed a heavy stare toward him and gestured him to do something, but he didn't. So she did.

'Please, please help us, Your Majesty?' Shelley pleaded... and there was a long pause.

'Majesty... I like that.' The voice seemed to mellow. 'Who are you?' The high-pitched tones rattled up through the void. 'You seem familiar to me.' The voice tried to recollect.

'I am not of this world, I am Shelley and I want to go home,' Shelley said with a plea of sadness.

'Don't be too sure about that,' the voice expressed and continued, 'What do you call home?'

'I live in another place, called Timpton,' she answered honestly and there was another slight pause.

'Timpton,' the voice reverberated from the depths of the fissure, 'M-m-m, what about your friend?' the heavy tones of the voice pressed on.

'He already said he lives in Reflections,' Shelley answered flippantly.

'Do not disrespect me, you insolent creature,' the voice boomed back in contempt.

'I-I meant no disrespect, I just don't know what you mean by my friend. I only know Kevin in this land,' she continued apologetically.

'I meant your friend, Katie.' The voice projected the news and Shelley was flabbergasted.

'How do you know of Katie?' Shelley quizzed.

'I know of everything,' the voice answered, 'Katie

followed you into Reflections.' Shelley's heart almost stopped, and a deep fear consumed her. She turned to Kevin, who had been standing silently, taking in all that was spoken.

'Who is Katie, Shell?' Kevin asked.

'Do not interrupt me,' the voice erupted in annoyance.

'I didn't mean to interrupt you, Your Majesty. I'm sorry, but I didn't know of this Katie,' he said apologetically.

'It seems to me you are both a little confused, you must work together to help your friend,' the knowing voice reasoned.

'I now have two problems, Your Majesty. I need to find Katie and we both need to get home.' Shelley portrayed her plight.

'You have more than two problems.' The voice hesitated. 'There is the evil one...'

'Shadrack Scarrat,' Kevin whispered under his breath, enough for Shelley to be reminded.

'...but also another!' The voice confirmed.

'Another besides Shadrack? Who is the other?' Kevin questioned abruptly.

'You dare once more to interrupt me.' There was a throaty wail from below and Kevin shuddered.

'I-I'm sorry, Your Majesty... I-I didn't mean to upset you.' There was silence for a short time and the voice continued in a calmer refrain.

'There is one place at which you and your friend Katie can get back to Timpton, and that place is Settlers' Bridge,' said the voice.

'I know where that is, Shell, it's the other side of Scarrat Town, on the outskirts of Reflections,' Kevin whispered, so as not to annoy the voice anymore.

'But you must be there on the 'Dawn of Reflections'.' Then the voice began to fade.

'But what is the 'Dawn of Reflections'?' Shelley called out, but the voice echoed away.

'You will know.' The answer melted into the darkness.

'What do I do at dawn? Or do I do it just before? Or just after?' Shelley pleaded, but it was hopeless as there were no more answers. In a panic Shelley searched around and found another stone.

'It's no use, Shell, it's gone, you won't get it back,' Kevin tried to tell her, but she had already launched it over the edge.

'Where is Katie? Tell me where she is?' Shelley screamed into the blackened void, but in doing so she overbalanced and toppled straight into the hole head first. In a snap reaction Kevin grabbed her leg just before she disappeared for good. She screamed and stopped falling with a lurch.

'Kevin... aargh... help me,' she whimpered from below.

'Stop wriggling and keep still or I'm going to lose my grip,' he protested. She calmed down as he asked, and he slowly reeled her in with all the strength he could muster. He dragged her over the ridge and she sat panting for a while. Kevin stood beside her and began laughing.

'What's so funny?' she sulked.

'Have you always been this clumsy?' he asked, still giggling.

'Yes, as a matter of fact... Okay,' she retorted. He could see she was annoyed and stopped his teasing. A moment later there was a curious low purring sound that seemed to emit from behind them, followed by a deep growl. Kevin and Shelley were still facing the void and looked at each other filled with terror. They turned simultaneously and there before them was the biggest, blackest panther either had ever seen.

'Oh my God.' Shelley mumbled, gulping in mouthfuls of air.

'Yeah' Kevin responded, 'This must be his hunting ground.' The beast was quite beautiful, if it had been behind glass in some zoo. Its short glossy fur was sleek and shimmered with a blue/black sheen. Its head was the size of a large pumpkin that eventually tapered off to the end of its snout. Great white fangs protruded from its upper jaw, like two tusk-like daggers, and its green eyes were lively and terrifying. The teenagers didn't move, couldn't, in reality. The panther slowly padded forward, each paw held razor-sharp claws. The beast was easily up to the height of Kevin's chest and the length of his whole body.

'Wh-aa-tt aaa-rre ww-eee goo-nn-aa d-ooo?' Shelley stuttered through clenched teeth, at the same time slowly edging backwards.

'For once, I have no idea, but don't go back any further, Shell. There's nowhere to go,' Kevin replied honestly, quietly and gravely. He turned his head slowly and saw the sheer drop of the void again.

Another growl from the beast rumbled the very rock they were standing on and Shelley let slip a scream from her lips. It seemed to move with a general purpose in mind and a flash of satisfaction glazed its eyes. The panther tensed, eased back on its haunches and sprang at them! As if in slow motion it sailed through the air and just as it got within a gnat's whisker of them, it halted! They instinctively put up their hands to protect themselves, screaming in their fear.

Unbelievably, a giant tongue-like vine shot up from the depths of the void. It sliced through the air like a huge whip, wrapped itself around the belly of the animal and plucked it into the sky. The captured panther flew over their heads, and had a look of sheer disbelief on its face. Kevin pushed Shelley over onto the ground and rolled away from the edge. The vine retracted and swallowed the beast into the bowels of the mountain. The voice of the void seemed to sigh in a satisfied gasp. The whole incident lasted only a minute or so. Kevin looked at Shelley and she stared back at him. They were shaking as if cold, but thankful they were still alive.

'That was incredible. Come on, Shell, we're not staying here any longer. Let's go before something else happens,' Kevin said, and gently lifted her back to her feet, 'We'll find Katie and get you both home, I promise.' Shelley, still reeling from the attack, reacted quickly and moved off immediately.

'What do we do now?' she asked.

'We've got until the 'Dawn of Reflections', which I thought was only just an old story. If it is true, then it's only a few days away. In the meantime, we must keep away from Shadrack and his Razzard Wolves if we are to survive, and anything else that might want to kill us,' he said recalling the recent attack.

'And whoever else is following us,' she said uncertainly.

'Yes, popular aren't we?' Kevin looked back at her and gave a nervous smile. Still reeling from the crazy adventure with the void and the near-death experience of the panther, they made their way down the twisting path of the gorge. The mist was rising from the heat of the day, but there was a cool freshness in the air.

'Will I ever find Katie? And will we ever get home? How on earth did she follow me, I wonder?' Shelley questioned herself.

'I don't know, but what I do know is that whatever it takes, I will get you home,' Kevin promised.

Chapter 12

Captured

Katie gently opened her eyes and instantly shut them tight again. She instinctively winced in pain. Everything in her body seemed to hurt and she began to sob. She gave herself a moment to pour out her emotions. A stream of tears made a white trail through the haze of dirt on her cheeks. After a while, she stopped crying and breathed in shallow breaths. The next move, literally for her, was to take stock of how much damage she'd done. Once she had flexed her limbs bit by bit, and gingerly wiggled her fingers to touch her face, she realised that she wasn't badly hurt at all. Her head was still aching, that was a given, but the thick mattress of fern she had landed on in the bushes had cushioned her fall. She took in her surroundings. It was full daylight, but she was shaded in undergrowth. Where was she? It suddenly dawned on her like a tidal wave of suppressed memory. The full weight of the accident came flooding back. She recounted the terrifying ordeal of the train speeding along the countryside. And her friend, the monkey, pulling at her arm to jump off and possibly miss the infinite threshold of death in the shape of the end of the track looming in the distance. That was why she was lying here, because Monkey had saved her life. But where was he?

'Monkey... Monkey, where are you?' She couldn't see him near her and he didn't answer her call. With all her might she lifted herself upright. It ached terribly, her stiffened limbs screamed out as a reminder of the fall. Once more she called, 'Monkey, where are you? Are you all right?' She leant forward and pulled the bushes to either side like a pair of curtains. It was at that point that she got the shock of her life... Plogs!

At least six of them were staring back at her, their tiny baby faces twisted and filled with anger. She screamed, and scrambled back as far as she could, but they were all around her. She also tried to get up and run, but it was no use, they were on her before she had any chance. She was captured!

'Get away from me, you sleaze-bags, get away.' She ranted and kicked and punched with all her remaining energy, but that was futile, too, against the might of the Plogs. Katie was too exhausted to fight anymore, and when she stopped, one of the blue creatures peered deep into her eyes. It was strange, but suddenly her head didn't hurt anymore, nothing hurt anymore. She felt as though she was in a wonderful dream, warm and cosy as if nothing mattered. She had succumbed to the peaceful world of hypnosis. Instead of struggling now she got up and began to follow the creatures in an obedient and quiet manner. A silly blank expression hung on her face, like a tranquilised animal. The sun was high in the sky and the power of its rays beat down with tremendous energy. There was so much heat irradiation in fact, that each Plog looked extremely uncomfortable. They walked along the dirt track that stretched on a parallel path to the railway line. The Plogs' eyes began to swell and bulge and each one's skin became flaky and dry. They gulped for air and a strange, sickly brown pus oozed from the cracks in their skin.

The group headed toward a concealed doorway further down the line. They travelled the route that depicted the railway track on one side and on the other the boundary of another wooded area that swept into the immediate distance. The path then veered away from the railway line and threaded through the outer edges of the woodland. Katie strolled in the centre of the body of Plogs, quietly roaming as if walking to school.

The bright daylight brought with it rising temperatures, which didn't sit well with the alien group and they became even more uncomfortable. They all longed to enter the shaded cover of the woodland and the eventual protection of the cool, dark underground tunnels. A crisp snap of a branch caught their attention for a brief moment and they stopped and peered suspiciously into the shaded forest. One walked over to the perimeter, gazed briefly and returned to the others. They moved on into the protection of the trees and little sighs of relief eased from their cracked lips.

Once the Plogs were shaded from the strong heat of the sun they relaxed.

Thud! One Plog instantly fell to the ground with a thick white liquid oozing from a gash on its shiny bald head. Thud! Another Plog collapsed to the ground and didn't move; a whitish liquid flowed from a cut and slowly seeped into the dried earth beneath. That was enough to bring Katie back to her senses. The ring of hypnosis was broken and the Plogs were in disarray. She felt a tight grip on her arm and realised that one of the nasty creatures wasn't going to let her go anywhere.

'Let go of me, you ugly cow,' she screamed and without thinking lashed out at the unsuspecting creature, punching it square in the face. The attack stunned it and it let her go and made for the doorway of the tunnels. In the midst of this, more stone missiles were sent flying through the air. The small group of Plogs that were left broke ranks and made a dash for the hatch, with at least one more Plog falling on their escape. The last of them quickly disappeared through the open door, leaving a hail of stones bouncing off the metal cover. Katie didn't know what to do. She was scared and confused, so she ran away as fast as she could. She sprinted out of the forest and down the dusty track in the opposite direction to the escaping Plogs.

'Stop... stop!' someone shouted from inside the woods, but Katie ran on. Soon there were more voices calling, so she glanced over her shoulder and saw darkened figures emerging through the trees. Her heart pumped faster and faster, making her breathing erratic. She picked up speed and soon lost them. She was very quick on her feet and burst into long strides across the rugged landscape. Eventually Katie stopped running when she could no longer hear anyone calling. She hid inside the hollow of a large tree that had decayed over the years and tried as hard as she could to keep her breathing quiet and shallow. There were voices calling from far away, but she didn't make any attempt to see who the perpetrators were.

She cowered deep inside the log quietly for a long while. The only movement was the expanding and contracting of her chest, which gradually became easier. No one had found her, not the Plogs, not even the strange people who had chased her. Her lips were dry and her tongue stuck to the roof of her mouth. Once she had swirled it round inside her mouth it moistened.

Her limbs became stiff after a while and it was then that she decided to take a look to see if it was safe. She agonisingly straightened her knees and squinted through a tiny gap in the bark.

It was clear. A smile filled Katie's dirty face and even that hurt a little. She stood upright and looked curiously beyond the point of the path; further out into the fields to the outer edges of the landscape something caught her eye. At first she couldn't make it out and rubbed her eyes to make sure she wasn't seeing things. But there it was, nestled between a group of overhanging trees; a small farmhouse. It was almost hidden because of the camouflage of creeping ivy that covered the whole building. It could just as easily have been missed. If it wasn't for the fact that there was a plume of smoke every now and then petering up through the branches of the trees, no one, especially the Plogs, would even know it existed. Katie was extremely drawn to the building, and now she was on her own thought that maybe she could get some help. Maybe even something to eat and drink. I wonder who lives there? she thought and, without any further ado, made her way to it.

She kept out of sight and crouched down along the hedges that led the way across the fields. Every now and then she would stop and dive to the ground and take a look around, just to make sure she wasn't being followed. It took a while to reach the overgrown bushes that guarded the little cottage, but eventually Katie was within spitting distance.

The farmhouse had a window at the front and one at the side, which were partly obscured with ivy. There was a heavy-looking brown wooden door to the left of the front window and a small porch roof. Katie then noticed a small window built into the roof, but with all the overgrown foliage it was almost impossible to see it. Now, should she just innocently walk up to the front door and knock or should she find out who lives there first? Katie sneakily crept around to the back of the building and saw there was another window there. She shuffled through the grass and lent underneath the windowsill with her back against the wall. She stopped for a short spell and admired the view from her vantage point. She could actually see for miles; it was the perfect place to stay hidden and keep an eye on the outside world, too. Back to the business at hand, she thought. Very slowly Katie slid up the wall to one side of the window, which made the leaves rustle in her ear. A wasp buzzed past by her face and made her jump, so she frantically swished it away! She eased over to her left and gingerly craned her neck until one eye peered inside. The window was too dirty to make anything out, but she could almost hear mumblings of a voice. There was a crack in the glass and a small piece was missing from the top right hand corner, but it was too high to reach. She could have climbed onto the sill and looked in, but she would definitely be seen. She tried to wipe the dusty pane of glass to see who was talking, but it was no use, all she could make out were shadows. What to do, what to do? Her mind was in turmoil. There can't be any Plogs in there, she reasoned, they wouldn't live in a farmhouse. That comment brought a little smile to her lips. All right, I'm going to have to go back around to the front. Katie grimaced at the thought. She didn't really want to do that, there was more chance of her getting caught, but she didn't have a choice. So she made her way to the front of the cottage, being very careful to keep hidden from the occupants of the house and anyone that was following her. In exactly the same way as she did at the back of the farmhouse Katie slid up the wall and turned her head to look inside. She grimaced at the thought of all the creepy-crawlies that must live inside the leafy world of the ivy.... As she was thinking that, something else took her attention. It stunned her at first, then she pulled away and slammed her back against the spongy surface of the wall. Was she seeing things? Rolling the thoughts round her head she made up her mind and turned again to the window. Katie pulled her sleeve over her hand to act as a duster and rubbed hard at the stained glass. Then she peered inside, but it wasn't her imagination at all.

'Good grief,' she mumbled.

Chapter 13

Mad Maisey

Katie's heart skipped a jump; there he was... her friend Monkey, and to all intents and purposes, locked up in a cage. She vigorously rubbed the glass to get a better view for clues as to why he might be there. What was she to do? She pulled back and rested against the wall, her mind working overtime. Think, think, think girl, she told herself.

Monkey wasn't having a good time at all. The little creature tugged and tugged at the bars, but couldn't break free. He was imprisoned inside the metal cage, which was suspended from the ceiling. He had never in his whole life ever been imprisoned before, and it scared him. Even in his time serving Lord Scarrat, he hadn't been tied up or locked away. This was surely different, this was the most terrified he had ever been. The person that had imprisoned him was the same person that had brought him there in the first place. Monkey remembered jumping from the train carriage, but the next thing he knew was waking up to find himself trapped inside a large dark holdall. When the holdall was zipped open, he immediately took his chance and climbed out. Thinking he was free, he tried to make a dash for it, but was soon recaptured. Without actually seeing his kidnapper, he was tied to the bars by a single tether to his right wrist inside the cage. When the kidnapper walked away, Monkey finally saw the back of her.

He looked around and saw he was in a small cottage with simple furniture. There was a small settee in the centre of the room, covered with rips and stains. Set in front of the window was a table and chair, and further over at the back of the house was a small kitchen. A pot simmered contentedly away on a dirty stove that had seen better days, and shuffling around the stove was the old lady. She seemed to be chopping up vegetables, busying herself ready for a meal. He felt hungry too, and his stomach rumbled at the aromatic odour of boiling vegetables.

The old woman had her back to him all the time, but he could tell from just studying her that she didn't spend much time using soap. Her long, matted grey hair settled rather than flowed onto her shoulders. She wore a shabby brown dress with dark stained patches that muddied even more whatever colour the dress had been. There were holes in various places revealing an even dirtier petticoat underneath. Her feet were clad in worn-out boots, with odd coloured socks which hung loosely around her ankles and looked as though they were trying to escape.

Monkey couldn't really move that freely, so he sat in wonderment and listened to the old woman; she was muttering something that he couldn't quite make out. On straining his ears to listen, it seemed she was singing her own little song. Every now and again she wiggled her huge backside in rhythm to the music of the song in her head. She giggled when she sang.

'Put him in a cage until I'm done, drop in the veg, tum tee tum tee tum, when the time is right I'll put him in the pot, then once he's cooked I'll eat the bloomin' lot.'

And every time she uttered the last words, she giggled some more.

Monkey rolled the words over in his head. Put him in a cage until I'm done. Drop in the veg, tum tee tum tee tum. When the time is right I'll put him in the pot... then it dawned on him! She's going to cook and eat me!

She continued repeating the same words, then suddenly turned to look in his direction. He'd somehow recognised her voice, but now with her staring directly at him it was apparent who she was, and Monkey stared back in horror, it was Mad Maisey!

Katie had turned back to the window. She could still see Monkey, but through the grime and dirt everything beyond the cage was just darkened shapes. One such shape, though, increased in size and overshadowed the cage. The taller and wider it got, the more Katie realised what it was. A large old lady emerged just feet in front of her and as the light caught her face it also caught the blade of a large carving knife. Her eyes were fixed and terrifying and blazed with madness. She seemed to look straight into Katie's eyes. Katie immediately dipped down under the windowsill, hoping not to have been discovered. She crouched in a ball, panicking, and waited for the front door to open, but it didn't! Her eyes darted around her head and her mind raced. She gathered courage and rose slowly up to the sill again and peered back inside. The woman was at the cage where Monkey was held captive.

Monkey scrambled as far back as the leash would allow, until he was almost tight against the bars. He stared into Maisey's eyes, his bottom jaw rippled with nerves. He remembered the day that he and his master had walked into town, that day of confusion, that day that this very same poor woman was being ridiculed in front of the town's people. The people had made a name up for her, Mad Maisey, due to fact that she usually ran around the town with her arms outstretched, flapping them like a bird's wings. That particular time, the kind Lord Scarrat had helped her, and openly showed his contempt for those that scorned her. But she had disappeared from the town since and hadn't really been seen after that.

Now, though, Mad Maisey wasn't flapping her arms like a bird at all. She was closing in on him, with a mad gleam in her eye and the glint of a knife in her hand. What made things even more eerie was the fact that she was singing as she approached him, but with a more sinister and insane tone!

'Put him in a cage until I'm done, drop in the veg, tum tee tum tee tum, when the time is right I'll put him in the pot, then once he's cooked I'll eat the bloomin' lot.'

But there was no smiling now; now only one thing was on her mind.

Outside, Katie was trying to figure out what to do and she didn't have much time to come up with a plan. Her mind was ablaze with all kinds of theories. Her nerves, though, were tighter than a violin string at the thought of clashing with this mad woman who was going to kill her friend.

Maisey, meanwhile, flung open the cage door and grappled clumsily inside for the main course of her next meal. She jabbed inside and sliced through his restraint with the blade. She eased out her knife and used her other hand to grab him, her fat grubby fingers flexed like an overweight spider. Monkey screeched and lashed out, using his claws, gouging at her knuckles.

'Then once he's cooked I'll... aargh,' Maisey screamed in pain and quickly retrieved her hand and sucked her fist. 'Oh, that hurt,' she sulked.

'Naughty, naughty monkey. Bad, bad monkey,' she squealed bitterly. 'I don't want to hurt you, little monkey, I only want you for my tea,' she said ironically, as a flash of murderous thought washed across her mind. Once more she fished inside, but this time she grabbed a firm hold and pulled him out, the crimson scratchmark clearly visible on her knuckle, from her previous attempt. 'Ha, ha. Gotcha.' She beamed in victory.

Katie gathered all her courage, reached for the door handle and burst inside the room.

'Put him down!' she bellowed commandingly.

Maisey was staggered to see someone else in her home and dropped the monkey and the knife instantly! When she saw it was a girl she narrowed her eyes and glared back at her.

'Get out of my house,' she raved, while she scooped the terrified animal back up in her hand and picked the knife up and held it threateningly to his throat. Monkey screwed up his eyes and tears forced their way out of the corners. His bottom lip trembled and he panted like a dog. He flexed his hands and wrapped them around the old lady's wrist in a feeble bid to restrain her. Her grip was powerful and her arms tensed.

'N-no, leave him alone, you-you can't eat him.' Katie reacted bravely as she raised her right arm and pointed her finger defiantly. This seemed to soften Maisey's spirit and for the first time she looked vulnerable.

'Why can't I?' she asked, but then it was forgotten about in a second. She made her way over to the boiling pot and suspended the trembling monkey over the scolding broth.

'No! Please, because, because...' Katie continued trying to think of something, anything.

Maisey turned curiously and faced the terrified school girl. Monkey meanwhile, hung like a slab of meat, sweating with the heat from the steaming pot and looking helplessly into Katie's eyes for some kind of help.

'Because he's not a monkey, he's-he's a...wizard!' she exclaimed.

'You're not foolin' me with that nonsense... he's no wizard, he's just a monkey and I'm hungry, girly,' she retorted in disbelief, and raised her knife threateningly.

Katie panicked for a moment and tried to think of something urgently. Then it dawned on her as if a light bulb exploded into life inside her head.

'Tell her, Monkey. Tell her that you are a wizard and-and if she doesn't put you down, you will put a spell on her, which will freeze her solid for the rest of time. Speak the words of wisdom, speak the words, Monkey,' Katie announced more boldly and nodded her head at what a good job she thought she'd done, hoping Monkey understood.

Monkey looked puzzled for a moment and then his eyes suddenly lit up, he realised what she was asking. In his deepest, darkest voice he said, 'Release me or you will feel my wrath.'

Maisey took in a deep breath, her face filled with amazement. Her eyes bulged and her mouth almost dropped to the flea-bitten carpet. Monkey could see she was taking it all in.

'Release me now, and I will spare your life,' Monkey said as sweat poured down his body and drenched his fur. Katie looked on in anticipation and bit her lip.

Maisey, humbled somewhat, slowly eased the knife away from the terrified monkey, gently laid him on the floor and placed the knife on the side of the cooker. Her face was a picture of confusion.

'Oh, no, no master. I'm sorry your wizard-ship, I-I didn't mean any harm, honest.' She looked rather sheepish, like a little girl, and began to cry. Monkey moved over to Katie and grabbed her hand.

'Now would be a good time to leave,' Katie whispered.

'Yes, I think you're right,' Monkey agreed. They left the old woman to her thoughts. The two of them edged toward the front door, not taking their eyes off the old hag.

'Please don't hurt me,' she sobbed.

'Never do this again and I will spare you,' the monkey said with authority.

'I won't, I promise,' she replied convincingly and with that, cheered up.

Katie felt a twinge of sadness for the old woman, but soon dismissed it when the thought of what might have happened if she hadn't intervened. Maisey sat by the table and buried her head in her hands. That was their cue, and they vacated the farmhouse and walked away as fast as they could. They continuously looked over their shoulder every now and again to make sure Mad Maisey wasn't following.

'Let's get as far away from here as possible, before she realises that we tricked her,' Katie confessed.

'What a brilliant idea that was, Katie. You're amazing,' Monkey confirmed with relish.

'Right, where next? We have to find Shelley,' Katie said with renewed determination.

'I have no idea where to start, but I'm not going back that way,' he said pointing in the direction of the train wreck. 'So, let's go this way.' He turned and Katie followed.

Chapter 14

The Stand-off

Shadrack was in a bad mood. His mind was full of turmoil over missing out on the two things he needed. He needed the book, which had been stolen from the Plogs that he had sent to retrieve it, and also the brooch that was fixed to the book that had gone missing, too. He really didn't know what the significance of the book was, but it must be important if it was connected to the brooch, he thought. The brooch and book, he believed, were stolen by two children, and he must find them to complete his plan. He'd even thought he'd had the two tearaways in his grasp at the Mud Flats; even that part of his plan had eluded him. He cursed himself for losing them in the curtain of steam that camouflaged their escape. Nothing was going his way and time was running out. He was really beginning to doubt his skills as a hunter altogether. When he was younger nothing escaped him on a hunt. Once he'd set his mind on pursuing the victim, he would eventually catch and kill it, but that was then. Now he had to take control and bring things back his way. The 'Dawn of Reflections' was fast approaching and he needed those articles to complete his ambition. Never mind, he thought, I'll have to put that to the back of my mind and get on with it. The day was serene and warm and in the hunter's eyes, unnerving. For the first time since leaving on his hunting trip, he felt alone and this is what sent his senses into overdrive.

His two wolves, Crusher and Ripper, had disappeared into the bushes in search of the teenagers.

Shadrack trailed behind, taking in all that surrounded him, looking for some clue as to where the young fugitives had gone. He turned to call on the Plogs that quietly followed behind, but to his annoyance, they weren't there!

'Of all the... where are they?' he grumbled under his breath. He swivelled his head around and still could not see hide or hair of his wolves either. 'Ripper, Crusher, where are you? You flea-bitten hounds,' he barked angrily. It was way too quiet and as still as a churchyard. 'Crusher, Ripper, get here now.' There was a long silence as he waited, only the slight rustling of leaves sounded as the wind played with them.

He sensed something, something strange and unusual in the air. Shadrak was a hunter and with years of experience, he knew there was something wrong. He lifted the strap of his rifle off his shoulder and, with eyes ever checking for danger, he broke the barrel open. There, as he had previously prepared, was a full chamber of bullets. This gave him an enormous feeling of strength and power and a broad smile lit his haggard features. The silence was marred, though, by a sudden yelping of his wolves. Shadrak quickly snapped his rifle back into place and eased back the hammer until it clicked. He was ready. He lifted the butt of the rifle onto the hub of his shoulder and stared down the barrel. He shifted forward, taking care to check his surroundings for any signs of trouble, pointing his weapon this way and that. He picked up speed and broke into a trot, keeping his head down and his senses sharp. The tails of his coat flared behind in the breeze and his boots kicked up small dust clouds as he scampered along the dry ground. Shadrak found himself in an opening amongst the trees and for one second cursed himself for getting into such an exposed position. He held his rifle rigidly, peering intensely now down the barrel and rotating in a circular motion at every conceivable attack point. The bleating of his wolves diminished and once again there was silence. His finger gently caressed the smooth metal of the trigger and his stomach tightened. Shadrack stood waiting for something to happen and a moment later it did.

From behind their hiding places the Plogs appeared. Shadrack flicked his gaze this way and that and found that they were everywhere, but what did they want? He was totally surrounded, a position every hunter dreads to be in. He bit his lip and cursed himself again; how could he have been so stupid. Then he reasserted himself, he wasn't going out without a fight. He kept his head and weighed up the situation.

'What do you think you are doing? I'm in charge here, like I've always been.' He spoke sternly and gritted his teeth.

'We do not take orders from you anymore.' One of the blue people stepped forward and issued the statement. Its baby face twisted in anger and its eyes black and deadly.

'You shall take orders from me, I am your master,' he reasserted his command. 'Now step back, before I lose my temper.' He pointed his rifle directly at the Plog who was talking.

'The only way you've been in charge is by the strength of your wolves, but they aren't a problem anymore,' another Plog commented. The hunter shifted his focus to the next Plog taking centre stage as he listened with venom pulsating in his veins.

'I am still in command, and you will listen to me...' The hunter's eyes widened and his nostrils flared, 'Where are my wolves? What have you done with them?'

There was no more conversation from the aliens and they began to close in. Shadrack aimed his rifle and fired two shots and two Plogs fell to the ground. A stream of white liquid pooled around their limp bodies. This stopped the Plogs for a moment, but once more they tightened the noose. Shadrack fired off a few more shots and more Plogs met their doom, but they moved in ever closer; there were far too many of them to stop with one rifle. He knew it was hopeless, but he stood firm all the same.

'Come on. Let's see what you're made of, eh?' he goaded defiantly.

The Plogs circled and stood off about ten feet away. They waited for him to try and reload, then they surged forward and were almost on him.

It was the first time in dealing with the Plogs that Shadrak Scarrat felt defenceless. He ranted like a wild man, trying with all effort to regain his standing as leader, but he could see it was futile.

'Come on, see if you can take Shadrack Scarrat, because I'm not scared of you, you useless alien scum,' he bellowed with an insane look in his eye and a grin on his distorted face. He used his rifle like a club and lashed out cracking heads. This course of action threw the creatures and they stepped back.

Shadrack quietened down for a moment and looked on in dumb curiosity. What's happening? he thought.

The Plogs weren't advancing anymore; in fact, Scarrat didn't know what they were doing. All around him were blue creatures clutching their heads as if trying to block out sound. Their faces were contorted with pain and a green liquid seeped out of the holes where humans have ears. Their eyes began to bulge and more liquid oozed from their noses. By now Shadrack didn't care what was happening to the Plogs, because they were retreating and disappearing into the woods, which was fine by him. Soon they were all gone and the hunter expelled a sigh of relief. Once more he was on his own and only the sounds of the forest filled his ears. Shadrack reloaded his rifle in haste. Why had they gone? Something had definitely hurt them badly enough, because Plogs never run from a fight, it wasn't in their nature.

Shadrack scratched his chin and then removed his wide-brimmed hat and scratched his head. Someone had just saved his life from the doom of the Plogs. He knew that without his wolves the Plogs weren't scared of him, and that's why they had killed them, someway, somehow. Why would anyone want to help him? And also, what weapon did they possess that kept the Plogs at bay? The thoughts tumbled through his mind. If they were helping him, then why didn't they show themselves?

'Come out and show yourselves, I would like to thank you personally,' he said and waited. He stood silent again, closed his eyes and focused his hunting skills. If anything out of the ordinary had taken place, then his keen hearing would soon find it. A snapping branch, or a rustling or brushing of leaves, or even the shuffling of footsteps through the undergrowth; but, disappointingly, there was nothing to report. These people are as clever as me, he thought. He did, though, feel a strange presence. It felt like a tingling, deep inside the pit of his stomach. It was something he hadn't felt for a long, long time and it scared him! A familiar yelping soon changed everything. Was that his wolves? Were they alive?

'I'm coming, boys,' the hunter shouted, his gravel voice cutting through the sounds of his whimpering hounds. A fresh excitement of great joy filled his whole being. 'Keep calling, boys, I'm coming.' He raced along the ground, heading for the place from where the sounds emitted.

Finally he found them, circling the base of an old well that had been long since forgotten. He almost felt as though he could cry and soon banished the thought with a torrent of abuse.

'You stupid, useless mutts. How did you let a load of baby aliens trap you like that, eh?' Shadrack ranted from above the well, but with a satisfaction inside. He scavenged the area, found a rotten log and dragged it along the ground and heaved it over the rim. He laughed manically as they dived out of the way of its descent and it landed with a resounding thud! The wolves quickly scampered to their freedom, but cowered as they reached the top. They clambered out only to be kicked up the backside with a hefty whack from their master.

'Let's go, boys, no hard feelings,' he laughed out loud and quickly changed to a more serious frame of mind. 'I must find that boy and girl... I need that book. But most of all, I need that brooch. We're on our own now.'

The wolves led the way and Shadrack followed them, carefully checking the ground in their wake. He did stop for a moment and sensed something, but it was only a lingering thought and he dismissed it and moved on. Well, if there is someone out there, thanks, he thought. They trekked out of the forest and onto a rocky area. The Razzard Wolves circled a patch of ground waiting for their master to appear, both whimpering with cries of excitement.

'What is it, boys? What have you found?' He panted breathlessly as he climbed the slope to find his two pets sniffing a particular muddied area. He crouched down to his knees and beamed a wide, satisfied smile. There it was, the evidence he had been waiting for. There were two sets of footprints, untouched in the mud; a pair of boot prints that had a smooth sole and next to them, a curiously patterned smaller pair of feet. They had a strange word written on them; the letters spelt out 'Nike', imprinted in the mud. Must be some kind of strange magic, he thought and rubbed his chin. Mmm, I'd better keep my wits about me with this one.

A feeling of satisfaction filled him to the brim now he had a warm trail to follow. This was a hunter's main aim in life. Scarrat was about to leave when he heard something that made him feel warm and fuzzy inside. Down in the valley rising to the heights of the mountain was the voice of Shelley. Her echoed tones were heard above the everyday sounds of the forest and gave away her and Kevin's position even better than their footprints would have.

'Crusher, Ripper, come on, boys, we've almost got them.' He beamed excitedly.

High up on a ridge overlooking Shadrack and his tracking wolves, a figure stood. Crouched enough not to be seen, and cunning enough to know he had just saved Shadrack's life. He should have killed him, but for some reason he couldn't...

Chapter 15

Feller's Junction

The fishing lake was calm and undisturbed as the sun's orb reflected upon its surface like a golden disc. They'd backtracked and travelled down from the 'Void' and gone past the fishing shack and further down to the lake itself.

'This is a really beautiful spot, Kev.' Shelley took time out to look across and admire the landscape. Kevin also stood and took in its memories. The water was crystal, like a huge window and the faint plop of fish could be heard in intervals. Its grassy bank encircled the perimeter and overgrown foliage dipped a green finger here and there.

'My father used to bring me here when he had occasional days off, and we'd fish for hours.' A curl of a smile lifted his tired face. 'The funny thing is,' he smirked again, 'we never in all the time he brought me ever actually caught a fish, but it didn't matter, it was nice just to spend time with him.' Kevin's features changed and he gave a look of discontentment. 'That was until everything changed.' His eyes steeled over and the bitterness welled up inside him. Shelley reached out and held his hand and it brought him back to the moment.

'Things will change for the better one day, Kev, believe it,' Shelley piped up, not realising the acoustics of the lake. Kevin laughed at the surprised look on her face as her voice's echoed tones rang out, as did Kevin's laughter.

'It's called 'The Lake of Thought', Shell, and they say whatever you want to say will become true one day,' Kevin said.

Shelley thought for a while and then belted out, 'I want to go home with Katie! … I want to go home with Katie! … I want to go hom…!' Her exploding plea boomed through the surrounding mountains and forests and up into the blue expanse.

Kevin felt a tinge of regret at Shelley's statement. He had become a close friend with her in the short time since they'd met and it really hurt him to think of life back on his own again.

'Come on, Shell,' he uttered quietly so it didn't re-verberate, 'if we go down this way we can follow the stream as it builds into a river, and maybe find your friend back in Scarrat Town at the bottom.'

Shelley could see the sudden sadness in his eyes and realised what she had said, but kept her feelings of friendship to herself. She knew if there was any chance of going home it was going to be hard enough for her to part later.

They moved downstream on the twisting trail that saw the trickle of the stream become the force of a river. It flowed at a leisurely pace and glistened in the summer sun. The day wore on and eventually they came to a wide expanse of water which was filled as far as the eye could see with huge logs.

'Where do we go from here, Kev?' Shelley asked.

'Well, if we take a left and follow this path, we will eventually end up back in Scarrat Town,' he said with a sense of scepticism. 'Katie could be in the town, hidden or captured.' He continued, 'We could sneak in and try and find her, but there are obvious dangers.' Shelley looked at him with fear in her eyes. 'There are the Plogs, they are everywhere. Then there are Crusher and Ripper, Scarrat's Razzard Wolves, and then of course there's Shadrack Scarrat himself.'

Shelley sat for a moment to collect her thoughts. There was a large flat rock to provide a 'thinking chair' and it was situated in the right spot to overlook the elegance of the water's edge. Gazing at the river temporarily took away the impending turmoil that troubled her thoughts.

'This is another fantastic place in Reflections, Kev, this country is truly wonderful,' she said overwhelmed by the scenery, 'What's this called?'

'What, this place?' He looked nonplussed at seeing the log jam a million times before and not feeling particularly impressed. 'Oh yeah, this is Feller's Junction, the lumberjacks chop down the trees and send them downriver to be made into... well, anything really,' he said, not really interested in the manufacture of wood.

Shelley continued to stare at the area of water that was completely obscured by the dense mass of timber. She had never seen anything like it before in her life. It actually looked like a carpet of brown rollers, each log tightly butted up against its neighbour in a pattern of basket weave. Kevin became agitated.

'Shell, we're wasting time here. If you want to find Katie we're going to have to move, and the closer we get to town, the more dangerous it's going to get,' he repeated.

'What's the matter, Kev? You seem nervous,' Shelley probed.

'It's too open here, we must move and find cover. Scarrat's spies are everywhere.' Kevin realised that he had become too relaxed, and being relaxed meant he wasn't concentrating and that meant that the enemy had one over on him. His worst fears were soon to be realised, sooner that he thought.

The pair were jarred back into reality by the sounds of snarling and howling. They turned and looked back toward the trail. There, gaining ground by every second were the Razzard Wolves of Shadrack Scarrat and they were heading in their direction. Behind them, Kevin could see a ragged figure with the familiar wide-brimmed hunter's hat and the almost devil-like form of the evil stalker.

'Shadrack Scarrat, good grief, he's found us,' Kevin winced. 'Damn,' he cursed.

'He's got us, Kev, it's too late to run,' Shelley relented with a fearful tremble in her voice.

'He hasn't got anyone yet!' Kevin reassured her. 'Come on.'

'Where are we going to go? Those dogs will be here any minute.'

Kevin looked deep into Shelley's eyes and then over to the river and back again.

'No-no Kev... I-I can't,' Shelley responded and stared unbelievably at the log jam. Two shots were fired from Scarrat's rifle, the blasts echoing through the valley. One ricocheted off the rock Shelley had just been sitting on and buried itself into the ground a little further over. The second blasted through the air, and hit Kevin on his arm. He let out a squeal of pain and fell to his knees, holding the wound. Shelley immediately realised what had happened and screamed hysterically.

'Kevin, you're hurt. Oh, God, it's bleeding.' Blood was slowly seeping between his fingers and soaking into his shirt. Kevin released his grip on his arm and assessed the wound.

'It-it's on-ly a graze I think, Shell... the bullet only clipped my arm, it's all right really, Shell, don't worry. We have to move now!'

Scarrat smiled and dropped the rifle to his side. I have them now, he thought.

'He's trying to kill us. He's really trying to kill us,' She repeated, totally amazed at the very real events that were taking place.

'I know, Shell. That's why we've got to head over the logs, it's our only chance.' Kevin got back on his feet ready to run, the red patch of blood clearly visible on his sleeve.

'No, Kevin, I can't, go without me,' she continued and pulled back, but he had already moved on and she had no choice but to move because she was already overbalanced. She found herself on the first log.

'Stay there, don't move!' Shadrack roared at the teenagers, his wolves obeyed immediately. 'Not you, you idiots. Get after them, they're getting away.'

By the time Ripper and Crusher were at the embankment, the two children were a quarter of the way across. Shelley couldn't believe that she was still upright, balance was normally on a par with her clumsiness, but she hadn't fallen in so far.

'Wow, I didn't realise how easy it was to walk on

141

logs,' she said with a spark of relief. 'They'll catch us if the wolves can walk on these logs, Kev,' she added.

'These logs won't stay like this, Shell, believe me.' Kevin spoke with experience and as soon as he uttered the last doomed words, it happened. The wolves dived on and the tightly nit cluster of timber slowly began to part company and rotate. Shelley was taken completely by surprise at the separation of the log jam.

'Kevin, they're moving,' she whimpered and began to move with them; it felt like peddling a bike.

'Keep it going, keep it going,' Kevin repeated.

By this time Shadrack himself was on the rolling carpet. Kevin kept his balance and urged Shelley to do the same.

'Just keep your balance and roll with it, Shell.'

The wolves had stopped growling and were concentrating more on staying upright than pursuing the fleeing pair. Each wolf gingerly padded his way across. Every log stepped on now was rolling and Kevin got into a rhythm of running and leaping to the next. (With all the excitement of escaping he'd forgotten about his arm for the moment). He was quite skilled and when Shelley had a second, which at this rate wasn't recommended, she flicked her attention to see how he was doing it. He looked at her and smiled.

'You're doing fine,' he said. Kevin was expert at it. He used to play touch with the other children on the log jam, when he was eight, much to the annoyance of the lumberjacks, so he knew how to handle the movement.

Shelley stepped onto one particular log and it slowly

spun and gradually picked up speed with the momentum of her trying to walk off it. The problem for her was, the faster she tried to step off the faster the log spun.

'K-e-v-i-n... I -c-a-n-'t stop!' she rattled.

'Slow it down, Shell, keep it under control,' he remarked, but the faster she went the faster and faster it went, without actually going anywhere... to the delight of Shadrack.

'I – can't – stop – it.'

Shelley was jogging on the spot and that in turn turned into a sprint. Her arms were flared out like a bird's wings in flight and her legs were speeding like a manic spider. How on earth is she keeping upright, Kevin pondered and gave a little smirk, even though they were in great danger. He then lost his concentration and his log began to spin out of control. The pair of them looked like they were competing in an Olympic event.

The hunter got so excited at the sight of the two teenagers trapped in one place that he stepped on two logs at the same time without thinking. Instinctively, his arms shot out and he thrust his pelvis back and forth, trying to keep balance. He resembled Elvis Presley in full rock mode and, if he wasn't having enough problems, his wolves were in even more trouble. Crusher was yelping for all he was worth, trying to stay up on all fours, while Ripper had two paws on one log and the other two resting on another... and the logs were separating! His eyes bulged out of his head and he gave out one last yelp, until he couldn't stretch his limbs any wider. Splash! Unprepared for the landing, he bellyflopped into the drink. Shadrack had calmed himself and managed to step onto another log and keep a more even flow. He was getting closer and closer and could almost touch them. The two teenagers were still at full pelt, but Kevin had jumped from his place and was keeping rhythm on Shelley's. Shadrack gave out a satisfied grin, because he was only two logs away from his victims.

Kevin managed to glance behind, peering over his shoulder briefly. He saw the impending doom of Shadrack Scarrat almost within grasping distance. He grabbed Shelley by the collar and surged forward. Shelley had no idea what was going on, keeping balanced was taking up her whole concentration, so when Kevin grabbed her she closed her eyes and hoped. In a twenty pace race the two runners flitted across the logs and didn't fall into any gaps. More by luck than judgment they skimmed across the logs, much like a pebble skimming across a still lake. When they got to the end they flung themselves off the river and onto safe, solid ground.

Shadrack lunged at the same moment as the two made their escape. He landed on the same spinning timber as they had just left. To his credit, he kept a steady pace and his sour jib changed to a satisfied smile. He looked directly at the pair panting on the bank and mouthed the words, 'I've got you now,' and that made Kevin and Shelley swallow hard. But that soon turned to laughter when Crusher appeared on the same log and took out both of them. They each plummeted into the cold lake. Shadrack spluttered and cursed at his dogs and at the two laughing teenagers, who got up and walked away in retreat.

'We must go quickly, Shell, because Settlers' Bridge isn't much further downriver and Shadrack falling in the river this end won't keep him away for long, he'll soon be onto us again,' Kevin said breathlessly and pointed where they had to go. They made their way up the banking and disappeared into the tree line.

'Kevin, stop for a moment and let me take a look at that arm,' Shelley pleaded.

'We haven't time, Shell,' Kevin retaliated.

'I don't care; I have to take a look at that arm.'

She was quite determined and Kevin relented. His sleeve was red and sticky, but the blood didn't seem to be flowing, so as best as she could Shelley tore part of the sleeve from her blouse. She wiped away the excess blood and found it was in fact a slight graze, to her utter relief. She then tore a strip from her other sleeve and expertly dressed the cut.

'You've done this before,' he commented curiously.

'We had a first aid person in school recently; I must have picked up some tips,' she said surprised at her own handiwork.

'First aid?' asked Kevin, slightly puzzled, 'Well anyway, thanks, Shell.' He smiled and inspected Shelley's nursing expertise. 'Hmm,' he uttered, and with that they walked further on.

Chapter 16

Settlers' Bridge

Monkey and Katie roamed from the farmhouse and into deep forest again. They were vigilant at every step. Monkey moved with uncertainty, as did Katie, for neither were sure of where they were going.

'This is hopeless, Monkey. Let's face it, I'm never going to find Shelley again, and I'm going to be stuck here for the rest of my life,' she said and her eyes welled up to cry.

Monkey could see how upset she was and waded in to lift her spirit.

'So, where you come from, do they give up this easily?' he said flippantly. 'You've just saved my life, so if you are capable of doing something as important as that, then getting home with your friend should be no problem,' he added smartly. Katie thought about it, stopped feeling sorry for herself and felt better after listening to the monkey's wise words.

'You're right, Monkey, I can achieve anything if I try,' Katie said reasserting herself and nodded her head in agreement.

'Let's find your friend and get you home, then.'

The little creature scuttled along the ground and shimmied up a tree to try and get his bearings. He balanced along a particularly long branch and perched on the end, holding onto an overhanging branch above his head. Katie shielded her eyes and could just make out his small figure high up in the crown of the tree. Monkey studied the landscape from left to right.

'Can you see anything from there, Monkey?' she questioned impatiently, and had to repeat herself, because he was so high the wind snatched away her voice before it reached him. 'CAN YOU SEE ANYTHING?'

'Well, I think I can see running water,' he mouthed in answer to her question without realising he was talking calmly to himself.

'Can you hear me, Monkey? What can you see?' Shelley called, again amplifying her voice in annoyance.

'Sorry...' he replied with more vigour, 'I think I can see a river, and something further over. But it's too difficult to make out from here,' he concluded.

'Well, you'd best come down and we can both move on and look together.'

'All right then,' he said, whilst still peering into the distance. Monkey slowly edged away from the end of the branch and moved toward the body of the tree. Still in mid-concentration he turned and misplaced his footing and fell off! There was so much foliage dressed around the branches that his free fall was hidden and unnoticed by Katie. He hit several branches on the way down to the bottom as Katie still gazed upwards.

'Where is he now?' she mumbled with impatience.

'Ouch... ouch... oompf... oooh.'

Katie was totally not expecting what happened next. As she innocently ran her eyes over the outside of the tree, a raggedy, misshaped missile landed plumb square on top of her and knocked her flat to the ground. With the wind knocked out of both of them,

Katie opened her eyes and sucked in a huge mouthful of air, as did Monkey who was on top of her. She heaved him off her and they lay there for a while, until their breathing became regular again.

'I thought Monkeys could climb trees,' she said patronisingly.

'So... did... I,' he replied with a sheepish refrain. Eventually they got up, and Katie followed Monkey's lead.

The sound of rushing water soon overpowered the rustling of the wind, and the two travellers made their way instinctively toward it. They came to an area of forest that overlooked a river. Monkey flitted onto an incline and crouched below the edge and Katie joined him.

'What is it, Monkey? What have you found?' Katie whispered with interest.

'Look,' Monkey said pointing to the flow of the river and the bridge that stood proudly over it. Katie was filled with excitement with the prospect of finding houses or a town.

'Come on, let's go and cross it,' she announced eagerly.

'Haven't you learned anything about this country yet, Katie?' he said damningly and shook his head, 'We wait, and if it's safe, then we go down and cross it.'

They hid for a while in the bush staring intently at the bridge. Light was beginning to fade and evening was waiting in the wings. Katie cast her eye on the structure; it was made of solid timber and looked as sturdy as an elephant. She studied it for a while and noticed one strange thing; it didn't touch the water in any shape or form.

'Look, Monkey, it's suspended. That's impossible. How can it hold itself up?' she questioned. The bridge was a half-moon shaped structure that seemed to start and finish each end of the river with no stilts or legs in between.

'That's got to be Settlers' Bridge, Katie. It's the bridge that the first settlers in Reflections built to get across the river hundreds of years ago.'

Monkey's short history lesson ended there, as there was a disturbance that sent the birds flying off from their nests. Echoed mutterings interrupted them, so Monkey and Katie shrank deeper into the bush and quietened down. From their vantage point they were camouflaged from sight, but could still see clearly the scene that lay before them. They recognised right away who the voice belonged to. It was the second time since meeting Monkey that Katie had come in contact with the hunter. He was ranting at the two wolves that were skulking ahead of him. Each of the wolves' heads was bowed and their tails were firmly tucked between their legs. The two spies looked on in disbelief. The figure that approached the bridge was dripping wet. Behind him he left a dark trail of water which was quickly soaked up by the dusty trail. His pets, Crusher and Ripper, were also soaked and they shook the excess water off with a flurry of shakes. Their normally shaggy exterior was matted and flat and they looked like a pair of oversized rats. Katie stifled a laugh and Monkey shot her a deadly glare, to which Katie immediately acknowledged the danger.

'You stupid hounds, why did you let those kids get

away?' he scolded.

Katie faced Monkey and was just about to say something. Monkey gave her another stern expression and placed his finger to his lips. She understood and held back on what she was about to say.

'Let's get over this bridge and maybe we could actually catch them up this time,' Scarrat said sarcastically as he boarded the first part of the bridge. The two wolves did not step onto the bridge, they were sniffing the air.

To Monkey and Katie's horror the angry wolves looked up in their direction. They began growling and moving toward the hideout instinctively. Katie clung tightly to Monkey and held her breath.

'What are you two stupid hounds doing now? This isn't the time or place to go rabbit hunting,' Scarrat said angrily. 'We have a job to do, so COME ON!' he barked.

The Razzards weren't listening to him, until they heard the click of the hammer on his rifle slot into place. The dogs flicked their ears and turned toward their master, who was pointing his rifle in their direction. A swift moment later and they were bounding over the bridge. The hunter was cursing and squelching behind them.

Katie and Monkey relaxed and gave a huge blow of a sigh. They peeled away from their hideout as the hunting group moved halfway over the bridge.

'They have found Shelley and the boy, we must follow them and find Shelley before he does,' Katie blurted.

'How are we going to get ahead of them without the wolves smelling us? They almost caught us then,' Monkey said sensibly. 'Don't forget, he is a hunter and does this for a living.'

'Well, what do you suggest then?' she asked sulkily and stared directly into his eyes.

'I don't know, Katie, I really don't,' he concluded with a frown, and with that they heard a yelping coming from below.

Katie dived to the edge, followed quickly by Monkey. Katie gulped a rather large gulp that almost choked her. Monkey stared open-mouthed and didn't speak. What concerned Katie was the fact that the wolves had turned and were howling and yelping as if curious about something. They could hear the hunter shouting at the wolves and pointing in Katie and Monkey's direction. It was a very animated conversation because Scarrat's arms were waving around like a windmill in a wind storm. All of a sudden he relented and lowered his arms to his side and gave a garbled command. The dogs understood at once as they leapt into action and broke into a sprint back across the bridge.

'Katie, come on, they're on to us.' Monkey was up and clambering away in the direction of the forest.

'But... how?' she asked blankly and then seeing Monkey speeding off, didn't need much encouragement and was soon hot on his heels.

The trees were a blur as she and Monkey hurtled through the rough terrain of the forest. Besides the rush of air forcing its way past her ears, Katie's heart gave a jolt when she heard the faint howling of the wild wolves in the background. This sudden fright gave a new lease of life to her limbs, and the shock of her pursuers made her speed up her pace. Way ahead she could just make out the monkey disappearing into the dense wooded glade. It was getting difficult to see, as dusk was taking hold of the land. Shaded areas were black, and the grainy vision of evening gradually impaired her ability to see. Another howl burst through overhead, and Katie knew they weren't far behind. The sound of Scarrat's wolves was quickly muted by the rasping dry voice of the hunter.

'There she is, don't let her get away, if you know what's good for you,' Scarrat bellowed, knowing full well that in a few minutes it would be impossible to track them in the fading light.

It was on the verge of darkness when Katie ran exhausted into the heavily overgrown woods. It also must have been the fading light, combined with her poor knowledge of the geography, which made her fall. But what ever it was, Katie crashed into a particularly awkward knotted bough that was hidden in deep swirling grass. She tripped heavily and went flying through the air, straight into the open mouth of a hole. She fell sightlessly into the pit and only took a few seconds to land on the soft earth at the bottom, ending up face down in a mound of moist dirt. She shook her head and spat out a mouthful of earth.

'Yuk.' Katie rolled her tongue over her teeth and spat again in a most unladylike fashion. An overwhelming aroma of soil and blackberry hung in the air. She slumped back against the damp wall of the ditch and waited for the inevitable to happen. She was too winded to call out, so she craned her neck and stared at the odd-shaped opening of her prison. She couldn't get out, it was way too high, but that wouldn't really matter once the wolves and the hunter discovered her; so she sat in silence.

She waited and waited and waited, but the wolves didn't come. Neither did the hunter. What was going on? she thought, they were right behind me.

The smell of blackberry was overwhelming in the pitch blackness. So Katie reached out her hand tentatively and touched a small vine of berries that clung to the wall of the pit. A flash of excitement filled her and she ate them hungrily, cramming the sweet, succulent fruit into her mouth and almost choking as she swallowed and drank the rich fruity flavour. She started to shiver as the temperature dropped. The dampness was seeping into her clothes and the cold against her skin made her shiver even more violently. Katie panted in intermediate gasps, with the presence of cold coiling round her. She rubbed her arms briskly and her nerves tensed, as wave after wave of icy cold air engulfed her body.

After what seemed like a very long time, movement from above disturbed her trance-like sleep. Katie flopped back her head and concentrated her eyes on the top. By this time she didn't really care if it was the hunter, or the bogey man. If either was going to kill her, at least she wouldn't have to suffer the intense cold anymore. She could see nothing, but could hear something sliding along the side. With all her might she squinted into the black and red pitch until she caught an eyeful of dirt. She immediately turned away, looked down and rubbed her eyes. She felt a numbed tap on the top of her head and something slipped to the side of her face. She reached up, almost petrified at what she might find, but thought that whatever it was, she couldn't escape it anyway. But she didn't feel in her heart as if it was dangerous. Her fingertips came into contact with something cold and smooth. At first she darted her hand away, then nervously in the black of night, closed her eyes and flexed her fingers. It wasn't a snake or a rat or an insect... it was a thick vine; someone was helping her escape. Well, what did she have to lose? Another couple of hours down there and she would eventually die anyway!

Chapter 17

Scatterbrook

After escaping from Scarrat and his ferocious Razzards, Shelley and Kevin were in open country. They stood in the middle of what was once a forest, but now resembled a sparsely wooded desert. The area was starved of trees because of the years of the work of the lumberjacks. Tree stumps were everywhere, like warts on a frog's back. The pair looked on in silence until Kevin uttered the first words.

'I hadn't realised how many trees they had used for the stuff people need.' He spoke softly. His eyes were filled with regret and sorrow. He just couldn't believe the devastation they had inflicted. Kevin thought of the place where he lived, with its rich green countryside, and now to this desolate page of Reflections history.

'It's the same in my world, Kevin. Wood is needed for so many things and our forests are heading the same direction as yours by the look of things.' Shelley sympathised. Things looked all too familiar, bringing back the memory of all those lessons that bored her in school about the environment. For the first time in her life she felt more grown up and responsible for the way Earth was slowly fading away. She was jolted back to reality by an anxious Kevin.

'We must keep on moving, Shell. Once Shadrack gets as far as Settlers' Bridge it won't be long before he's onto us.' He gave a deep frown and concentrated hard. He rolled his head from side to side, studying the land, and noticed a winding track a little to one side.

'There's a road over there.' He pointed to the area and Shelley followed his direction.

'Where does that lead to?' she asked without thinking.

'I have no idea,' Kevin answered honestly, 'But wherever it goes we'd better go, too.'

The daylight was slowly drifting into evening as the wide expanse of blue was being infiltrated with a mass of cloud. Shelley and Kevin walked down the bumpy hillside and onto the gravel road at the bottom. It flowed in two directions, but Kevin didn't want to backtrack, so he faced the way uphill. The road was wide enough to accommodate traffic and there were wheel tracks grooved into the surface.

'There must be people here, maybe they can help us.' Shelley beamed with her first ray of hope since she'd entered Reflections. 'Which way shall we go?'

'I'm not going that way. Shadrack might be making his way toward us from there,' Kevin said, pointing downhill. Shelley wandered on up the road by herself.

'Hey, wait for me,' Kevin called out and skipped up beside her.

They walked a few miles and kept a check behind just in case they were being followed. The light was fading as they rounded another bend, then they saw a cluster of buildings over the next hill. Kevin's first reaction was to grab Shelley and disappear behind the nearest clump of bushes. Shelley was getting used to being pulled in all directions and hiding, and thought nothing of it.

'What do you think?' she whispered. Kevin didn't

answer for a time; he was concentrating on the outer buildings of the town.

'Kev, wha...'

'Shh...' He pressed his finger to his lips without looking in her direction.

Shelley did as she was told, but folded her arms in protest. 'I'm not stupid, Kev,' she rambled in an even lower tone.

'Sorry, Shell. But I'm trying to think.'

The town was still a fair way off, but from where they were looking there didn't seem to be any movement. Kevin looked harder, but couldn't make out any people. The road slipped in between the houses and there were taller buildings that stood out from the others. The light was ebbing away fast and Kevin knew he had to get there with Shelley while they could still see.

'There can't be anyone living there, Shell, not from what I can see anyway. It looks pretty peaceful.'

'How do you know? It's getting dark. No matter how good your eyes are, Kev, it's too difficult to see anything in this dim light. Maybe there are people there who can help us,' she expressed angrily. She was right and Kevin knew it.

'All right, then, let's go there and see for ourselves, and if it's empty we can hide until morning. Perhaps we can find some food.'

With that Kevin's stomach rumbled and Shelley giggled, until hers rumbled too and her face soon reddened. By the time they actually got to the town it was completely dark. Kevin reached into his trousers and pulled out a small rubber torch that was zipped in an inner pocket. He switched it on and a small beam of white cut into the darkness.

'How long have you had that?' Shelley asked curiously.

'All the time, I'd just forgotten it was there,' Kevin answered sheepishly, remembering the times he could have used it before. He raised its frail beam and it rested on a wooden sign. 'SCATTERBROOK' was the name of the town. Its flaky paintwork had peeled away part of the 'S' and 'K', but it was still legible.

Shelley and Kevin entered the perimeter and kept to the centre of the track. There were no street lamps or lights of any description to help illuminate the way. There were buildings and houses each side of them, but they were hidden in the dim settings. Kevin's torch light reflected off a window or a white painted porch post to remind him he was actually in a town. They eventually came to a crossroads. Kevin pointed his torch in each direction, but it was too dark for the beam to make a difference. They were dead centre of the town. Shelley shivered.

'Why aren't there any people? This is really strange,' Shelley remarked with a hint of curiosity.

'The Plogs must have come here a long time ago, and like Scarrat Town, everyone has either been killed or escaped,' Kevin concluded.

'It's cold, Kev,' Shelley uttered through chattering teeth, and tucked her hands under her armpits to keep them warm.

'That house looks okay; let's see if it's open.' He walked toward the entrance and pointed his torch at the door of a large white house, but before he could go any further Shelley grabbed his arm.

'What's the matter now, Shell? Like I told you, there's no one here,' he rasped impatiently.

'But what if there is? Come on, let's go, I don't want to stay here.' She beckoned impatiently.

'I thought you wanted to find some help in this town?' Kevin questioned bluntly.

'Look, Kev... I'm frightened,' Shelley continued whilst squinting at Kevin in the blackness and still walking forward. She then inadvertently tripped over the edge of the porch. She tumbled head first into the door, smashing it open with a clatter, and landed face down on the floor inside. She quickly righted herself and stared directly into the beam of Kevin's torch light.

'Are you all right, Shell?' he asked concerned, his face hidden behind the blinding beam. Shelley felt really embarrassed at originally trying to be quiet and trying to stop Kevin from entering the house. She had failed on both counts. The sound of her head hitting the front door was bad enough, she'd made enough noise to wake the dead; but Kevin had entered the house, anyway, to see if she was okay, which was what she had been trying to avoid in the first place.

'Well, if there is anybody living here, they certainly would have heard that,' he chuckled.

Shelley rather grim-faced, dusted herself down, cursing quietly in the process. 'What now?' she asked meekly with a quaint smile.

'Well, it's pointless backing out now, we're already inside,' Kevin said patronisingly.

'We may as well go in the rest of the way, now,' Shelley lashed back, with an overwhelming wave of attitude.

'Great, I'm starving; perhaps we can find something to eat in here.'

Shelley didn't argue because she was hungry, too. The small circle of light from Kevin's torch hovered along the inner porch wall and glided over a vast painting which depicted a large cat. Its eyes flashed when the beam caught the canvas and made Shelley jump. She let out a gasp of air. Kevin almost did the same, but he kept his composure. He pointed the light along the rest of the wall and it suddenly got swallowed up. There was a huge gap that opened up onto the stairs. He and Shelley stepped closer and he shone his tiny torch up the winding stairway. Everything looked spooky and still.

'I don't like it in here, Kevin, let's go, please,' she whispered to him as he tilted back his head peering onto the darkened landing.

'Look, Shell, it's warmer in here and safer... and if there's food as well.' Kevin brought the light back down and pointed it so she could see him shrug his shoulders. He was right and she knew it. It was warmer inside, but it didn't make her feel any easier. He continued to drift its light along the foyer until it rested upon a shiny brass door handle.

'There, through that door. There's sure to be food on the other side,' he proclaimed proudly with a hint of real excitement in his voice.

As they approached the door the whitish beam shimmered on the handle until Kevin grasped the cold metal and gave it a twist. It clicked and fell open quite freely, giving a screech of freedom from its rusty hinges. There was a long hallway behind it, and where Kevin's light landed was yet another door. Kevin's heart sank, how many more doors would there be before he could eat? He asked himself.

Their echoed footsteps on the hard tiled floor cut through the otherwise overbearing quietness. Kevin gently reached out once more to grab the next doorknob. He tentatively caressed the handle and stopped! Both he and Shelley stood stark still and listened! At first they couldn't hear anything, but then with both pairs of ears straining for sound, it came again. There were padding footsteps coming from overhead. Shelley almost screamed until Kevin put his hand over her mouth and made a motion with the shake of his head. Kevin urgently lifted his torch and aimed it upwards at the ceiling and ran the beam along the route of the mysterious footsteps. Shelley pulled away his hand and panted.

'There's someone here, let's get out quickly,' Shelley squeaked.

'It's too late for that,' Kevin said with an air of finality, 'They're coming down the stairs, we have to hide.'

'Let's just go out the way we came in and run outside so they can't find us,' she protested.

'It's definitely too late now, Shell. Whoever it is, is halfway down the stairs and would catch us before we even made it to the front door. Let's go through here and hide inside until we can escape,' he said, and with that turned and pushed the door open.

They ran inside with Kevin feverishly searching with his torch, which by this time began to resemble a light sabre from a 'Star Wars' movie. Shelley closed the door quickly behind her and bounded after Kevin. Kevin sharply glided the beam over a work surface. The white light caught the glint of three neatly placed glass pebble ornaments that were set in the centre. There was also a clock that ticked harmlessly on the wall, and the ominous drip, drip, drip from a leaky tap. It was indeed the kitchen, and the back door was only a short distance away. Shelley was following closely behind now, and felt a jolt of relief at seeing the light reflect from the wooden panelling of the back door. Kevin gripped the handle and desperately twisted it in the hope it would open, but to their dismay it was locked. And to add a chill of disappointment, there was no key in the lock.

'Oh, Kev...' Shelley winced and felt like she wanted to cry.

The footsteps were now at the foot of the stairs, and sounded even more foreboding as they slowly approached the teenagers' direction.

'Kevin... what do we do? What do we do?' she repeated, gulping in air trying to speak at the same time. Kevin stood firm and looked back at her.

'There's nothing we can do...' he said calmly and searched for something he could use for a weapon.

Chapter 18

The Stranger

'Who's there?' Katie called out tentatively into the bleakness. It could be someone helping her, or it could be a trick. At first there was a pause, and then a stranger's voice tumbled down the hole.

'Grab the vine, I won't hurt you.' Katie could see absolutely nothing. It was as dark outside the hole as it was inside her gloomy prison. She could tell it was a man from the depth of his voice. Katie tried with all her focus and concentration to visualise the stranger; it was too dark to make anything out. His voice was that of an older man, she could tell by the quiver in its tone, but it was impossible to make out anything else. If it wasn't for the fact that the chilled breeze visited her at intervals she could swear that the pit was sealed.

'Who-who are you?' she called in a more firm voice, trying to find out more before she came face to face with the stranger.

'Who I am doesn't matter, all you need to know is Shadrack Scarrat and his wolves are gone.' His soft voice gently evaporated into the thick night air. This comment made her a little more confident. But was he lying? She had to make up her own mind.

'How do I know you won't harm me?' She waited anxiously for another answer.

'If I wanted to harm you, I could come down and hurt you just as easily as pulling you up, don't you think?' The faceless voice continued sarcastically, 'I want to help you, so hurry up just in case the wolves come back.'

Katie didn't answer for a moment; she ran the thought over in her mind. There was silence from both parties, but then after weighing up the fact that the man could have quite easily, if he'd wanted to, come down unannounced and done her in, she relaxed completely and gave in.

'Okay, you can pull me up,' she relented and the stranger didn't answer and began to tug at the vine. Katie gripped it with both hands and held on as tightly as she could. The vine began to lift her off the ground. She was being pulled up in slow, gentle stages.

'Oh-uh, I'm slipping,' she cried, and with that the two metres or so that she had risen soon reclaimed her as she once more hit the bottom. She puffed heavily and scolded herself for being so frail. It was the vine; it was wet from the dew and therefore very slippery. She began to shiver again as the cold wet earth clung to her clothes.

'Tie it around your waist and I'll pull you up again,' the stranger said, so Katie did as she was told and wrapped the vine around her waist, tying it in a firm knot.

Gradually in jerky movements, her body was lifted to within the neck of the hole. She became very nervous; it was horrible, like being pulled into some sightless doom.

'Give me your hand.' The voice was closer now. Katie was scared and hesitated, 'Come on, I can't hold this vine all night.' The stranger winced as he strained with her dead weight. She reached out and suddenly felt the warm strong hand of her rescuer. In the next moment he had lifted her completely out of the hole and onto the ground besides it.

'Are you all right?' he asked genuinely.

'Ye-es I think so,' she replied, but with a nervous twinge in her stomach. It was still blindingly black on the surface and the two figures couldn't see each other. The stranger shuffled around and about her. Her shivering became uncontrollable and she shook violently.

'Wh-at ar-e yo-u do-ing?' she stuttered suspiciously and with that there were sparks of blue and yellow light. Soon there was a flame, and the man had a fire going. 'Wha-t are y-ou doin-g?' Katie repeated frantically. 'They'll come and find us if they see the fire.'

'Don't worry about them coming back, they won't,' he said positively.

Katie moved closer to the bright flames and toasted her hands. The sudden warmth was welcoming even though it had only just begun to build. She relaxed some more and her voice came more freely.

'How do you know? How can you be so sure? You told me to be quick on getting out from the pit in case Shadrack came back. So how can you be so sure that he's not coming back now?' she quizzed suspiciously, the flickering flames dancing in the reflection of her eyes.

'Because they've gone after the two teenagers; I know because I've been following them for days. I only told you that to get you out of the pit,' he added.

The stranger had had his back to her, and now, with the fire burning brightly, he turned to Katie and she could see his face. The yellow flames reflected sharply in his eyes, too, and the continuing glow brought out all his features. He had a long, narrow, aged face which revealed deep pockets of black shadow under his eyes. His old loose skin and tired eyes in many ways reminded her of her grandfather's. His frame was also slim, even though he was now hunched up over the fire; his long slim fingers toyed with the twigs as he arranged them for the best result to catch the flames. He wore a suit coat, and trousers of a lighter shade that were darkened and dirty at the knees.

'Who are you?' Katie asked.

The stranger opened his mouth to speak, but didn't have a chance.

'Lord Fairbourne Scarrat,' the answer came, but not from the person sitting by the fire. Katie recognised the voice straight away, and Lord Fairbourne turned to the source. Immediately, Katie's heart burst into a drum roll and her face lifted to overwhelming glee. Lord Fairbourne smiled, a genuine warm welcoming smile, as out of the shadows and into the light came Monkey, small and a bit frazzled at the edges, but fine none the less.

'Monkey, is that really you? And you can talk! How did that happen?' the old man asked, and his heart danced with excitement.

'Yes master, it is me. It's a long story that I promise I will tell you some day.' Monkey smiled back gleefully, and immediately flung his arms around his master's neck and hugged him to the point of strangulation. Katie, although happy to see the two figures reunite, also felt a twang of jealousy.

'Oh, ho... how are you, boy?' Lord Fairbourne cried

with relief at seeing an old friend after many years of absence. They released from their embrace and each sat around the roaring campfire.

'How did you get away from Shadrack, Monkey? I lost sight of you.' Katie asked.

'It wasn't easy, but he was after you at first and that gave me time to escape. I figured if he did capture you, then I would wait for an opportune moment and rescue you. I looked back again and you were gone.' Monkey then gave Katie a huge hug, which made her feel loved again.

'Master, you must tell me everything of your adventures,' Monkey said with intrigue, 'Why did you leave master? Was it because the power was too much?'

'There were some other reasons, reasons I can't explain now, Monkey. We have no time to reminisce. I have a job to do, and that job is to stop Shadrack from getting the brooch. Once he possesses it he has the power to move to other worlds, especially as it will be the 'Dawn of Reflections' soon and that will be the point in which he can leave Reflections and wreak havoc anywhere he goes.' Lord Fairbourne was staring deep into the heart of the fire as he spoke.

Katie listened to the conversation that was taking place and realised something important. She eased back from the flames unnoticed by the two old friends.

'Shadrack is your son, isn't he?' Katie eventually slid into the conversation.

'Yes, that's right, he is, you are very observant, young lady,' Lord Fairbourne answered honestly.

'My friend Shelley is with the boy, I think. I must

find her and we must go back to our own time. But what happens if Shadrack Scarrat finds them before we do?' she asked solemnly.

'We have to try and not think about that, let's just make sure we find them first.' His face took on a more serious streak.

'And the Plogs? Don't forget the Plogs, master. They are just as dangerous as Shadrack and his wolves,' Monkey said, remembering the other lethal part of the problem.

'There is no need to worry about the Plog creatures. I have dealt severely with them,' Lord Fairbourne announced proudly.

'What do you mean, master? What have you done?' Monkey probed and Katie listened intently. 'I don't know how really, but I simply needed the Plogs to go,' he said, taking his mind back to the fight they'd had with Shadrack. 'Where were you, master, when the Plogs attacked you?' Monkey continued.

'They didn't actually attack me.' Lord Fairbourne paused, 'They were attacking Shadrack at the time.'

'And you stopped them? Why, master?' Monkey couldn't believe what his old master was telling him. Katie still listened intently in the shadows.

'Because he's my... son, I suppose.' Lord Fairbourne's face saddened. Monkey realised then how difficult a decision it would have been.

'But master, how did you get rid of the blue demons?'

'I simply wished them to stop harming my son and they began to die,' he said with actual bewilderment.

'It seemed that the power of Reflections mixed with my mind and finished the Plogs once and for all. They are all gone, presumably back whence they came.'

'You mean, master, that you just thought the Plogs away?'

'That's exactly what happened. If it hadn't happened to me I would never have believed it.'

Lord Fairbourne reached out into the darkness and picked up his shoulder bag. He fished inside for something to eat. He had sandwiches, fruit and a flask of tepid tea. There was also one object inside which he pushed further into the bag... a book. He unwrapped the cellophane and gave two sandwiches to Katie, which she received with bulging eyes, even though they were slightly stale around the edges. He kept the other two sandwiches for himself and gave the two apples, banana and orange to Monkey. Katie was also grateful for the warm tea. It felt good to eat and drink and Katie almost choked swallowing.

'Take your time, girl. You don't want to kill yourself and miss all the action tomorrow,' Lord Fairbourne chuckled.

'S-sorry, I was starving,' Katie spluttered.

'Let's all try and get some sleep, it's only a couple of hours until dawn,' Monkey said, throwing the last of the orange peel to one side. Then he curled up in a ball.

'Very well, Monkey, we sleep then rise at first light. This is the last dawn before the 'Dawn of Reflections'. We must help your friend and the boy, and stop Shadrack as well. Sounds an easy plan, eh?' Lord Fairbourne lifted the conversation with a smile and winked at Katie. 'These old bones weren't made to sleep out in the open. I'm way too old for this camping lark,' he grumbled as he tried to get comfortable on a dried patch of grass in front of the fire. Monkey just shook his head and grinned, happy to see his master again. Katie rested her head on Lord Fairbourne's bag and let the fire heat her back.

'Monkey, was that you?' Katie shouted in disgust.

'Sorry, Katie, it slipped out,' Monkey replied.

'Come on now, we have a lot of work to do in the morning and our very lives depend on it. One more like that one Monkey, and if it catches the fire the whole forest will be ablaze,' Lord Fairbourne smirked.

They all lay in front of the campfire and tried to drift off in dream, but the ground was hard and cold and their minds were full of dread. The hours drifted slowly away and the first break of light brought on the reality of what lay ahead. This was the 'Dawn of Reflections'.

Chapter 19

Closing In

Shadrack Scarrat had finally given up on his search for the girl. His mind was in turmoil. Where had she come from? She seemed to be dressed in the same sort of clothes as the other one, but it wasn't her, she had different colour hair. He immediately dismissed her from his mind. My main goal is to get the brooch from the boy and girl that I've been following; this one is of no consequence, he thought. His wolves had lost the scent in the woods; he knew time was running out for his escape from Reflections. He was losing confidence in himself more and more. Every time he had come close to his prize he had lost it again. What was happening to him? When he was younger things were easier. Whatever he followed, he would certainly catch up with and kill, eventually. But these were only children, a boy and a girl. Why was he having such problems? It's just a bad phase I'm going through, he asserted. I can't let this get to me, he reasoned. If my wolves get wind of my difficulties, I'm finished.

Shadrack came back to reality and began to think hard. He had an idea. Once he had got hold of the brooch, then he could use it to gain passage through the moment of the 'Dawn of Reflections,' and from there he could do whatever he wanted. It was a long shot, but Shadrack was sure that the power of the diamond, combined with the mysterious event of the 'Dawn of Reflections', would be enough. He shrugged his shoulders as if to rid his troubles away and re-aligned his thoughts.

He and his pet wolves left the woodlands far behind,

and the three figures walked over Settlers' Bridge and beyond. He was tired and his feet ached and he longed for a lie down and rest, but he couldn't stop, not now, he was too close. He was at last on the road that led far beyond the province of Scarrat Town and in the right direction to find the two fugitives. In a pocket in his bag, rolled up in a cotton cloth, was a strip of salted beef. He bit into it and tore off a small chunk and chewed it. It felt like he was chewing the sole of his boot, but it was the only thing he had time to eat. So he grumbled as he chewed and his face showed his disgust. He rolled the rest back up in the cloth and placed it back in his bag.

They were on their way to Scatterbrook; a town Shadrack knew was almost deserted, except for the one person he could count on to help him, if he was still there. It had been decimated by the notorious Plogs when they had arrived in Reflections, but now they were gone, and a wry smile curled his haggard face. The majority of the population of Scatterbrook had been killed, but a few lucky souls fled up into the hills. The same satisfied smile played on his lips as he thought of the idea of the teenagers entering Scatterbrook and hiding there.

'They are in Scatterbrook, boys, I can smell 'em.'

This seemed to spur the wolves on and stir up their already overexcited nature. He chewed the last part of his snack and gave a wince of disgust at the dull taste. The two wolves were hungry, too. They also hadn't eaten for quite a while and anxiously waited for their next meal. Shadrack knew they were ravenous and also knew they wouldn't be much good to him in a fight if they were too weak.

He had been keeping a lookout and finally, in the open countryside of the felled trees, he could see the answer he was looking for. He took the opportunity with relish at being a hunter. He swiftly unhooked the rifle off his shoulder, aimed it in the direction of a nearby glade and stood and waited until it was just the right time. His hand was steady and his eye true, he felt it in his gut what was going to happen next. Within seconds Shadrack cracked off two rounds and laughed out loud; he hadn't lost his touch at all. The wolves immediately turned their attention to their master, knowing instinctively what had just taken place; a flicker of excitement filled their eyes.

'There you go, boys. That should keep you happy for now.'

At the edge of the glade, now silenced after innocently playing together, lay two slaughtered rabbits. Crusher and Ripper took the signal and eagerly bounded across the grassy forest, each trying to outrun the other. Their cries and yelps echoed across the plains. It didn't take them long to pinpoint the fresh meat and they tore into the flesh, each trying to take more than his share. Their instinct took over and they snarled and growled and snapped at each other. Shadrack let them alone for a short while and then called out after them.

'Stop fighting, otherwise I'll personally kill you both,' he snapped through gritted teeth.

Both wolves lifted their heads, finished what they were doing, and obediently ran to their master. They circled him in respect, both wolves' teeth and jaws ran red with the fresh kill, and then they bounded off again.

It was fully dark as they walked the winding dirt road to the quiet little town. The last remnants of daylight had evaporated in the fruitless search for the fugitives. The thick veil of night was illuminated by the glow of the small oil lamp that he carried.

The devilish reflection of his wolves' eyes from the glare of his lamp brought his hunter's instinct back to him. They had stopped just ahead and both glanced back to their master. He knelt at their side and held his light above the ground. There it was, the one thing he had hoped for; footprints. They were the same ones that he'd seen in the dirt on the rocky mountain. He beamed a broad grin; the flame of his lamp depicted every deep line and crevice. 'I've got you now,' he mumbled. The wolves alerted him again with whimpers.

'What is it, boys? What have you found?' he rasped with irritation. He lifted the lamp up above his head and strained his tired eyes and saw the shadowed outbuildings of Scatterbrook town. The whole area was indented against the bluish black background of the night sky. The town stood tall and silent. Shadrack stopped for a moment and put his lamp on the ground. He retrieved a canteen of water from his rucksack and unscrewed the top. The old hunter drank thirstily and gulped huge mouthfuls of cold water until he was satisfied. He then took his rifle and reloaded it ready for action. His wolves were excited and at the ready.

'Shhhh, you mangy mutts, I don't want them to know I'm coming,' he whispered. He took hold of his lamp, doused the wick and the golden flame died. They were all plunged into darkness. Shadrack felt the cold steel of his rifle barrel, gripped his hand on the hub and clicked back the hammer. The smooth wood of the handle gave him a renewed confidence. He held it up and kept it at close quarters, pointing it at any sound or movement. He walked past the outer buildings that looked as though they were guarding the town, tall and foreboding. Inside his stomach turned; even he was nervous, for the first time in his life. He fought against his ailing weakness and took control once more.

'Crusher, Ripper, let's go find them, boys, but keep quiet,' he hissed, but the wolves had been in this scenario many times and knew exactly what to do. The old hunter scrambled along the dusty road waiting for some kind of sign. Each wolf took a separate side of the street and ran along the front walkways. Shadrack Scarrat took to the centre and as swiftly as he could, moved along behind them. Apart from the scampering paws of his beasts and the shuffling of his own feet, there were no other sounds. Being an old hunter he kept his eyes and ears open for any kind of clue. A sudden sweep of cold wind dusted his face with grit and he stopped to wipe his crusted eyes. Where are they? Where are they? He kept rolling the question over in his head. They've got to be here, I'm sure of it. Shadrack was beginning to doubt himself. His old instincts as a hunter of many years began to evade him. But his faith was soon richly restored!

They came to the crossroads and there it was, in the upper window of one of the houses, a brightly lit yellow lantern that was left there purposely. A warm prickly excitement filled his stomach. The same feeling he had had earlier when he held the rabbits in his sights before the kill. This is what he'd been waiting for, it was all he needed and he headed straight for it. 'Now I've finally got you,' he mumbled.

'Crusher, Ripper,' he whispered, and the wolves knew with the urgency and quietness in his voice that their journey was nearly over. They came to his side not excitedly now, but stealth-like. They were trained killers and followed their master as he led the way. Shadrack gripped his rifle tightly in readiness and made his way to the house.

Chapter 20

Davenport

Things couldn't have been any worse for the two trembling teenagers. They were trapped in a strange house and whoever owned it was now making their way to the kitchen to where the youngsters had dead-ended themselves. The footsteps were heavier and more prominent, and with the echoed thud on the flooring came shallow breathing. More like the rasping breath of the Grim Reaper. Kevin couldn't find anything that would resemble a worthy weapon, so he stood firm. Shelley panted like a dog that was hot from a long run. Her eyes were bigger than the dusty dinner plates that were displayed on the wooden dresser. Kevin gently guided her behind him in an act of chivalry, and focused the fading light of his torch at the door. His lower jaw began to quiver and his hands were shaking. The white beam was trembling, so he had to try to calm his nerves to steady it.

'When the door opens, we'll rush at it and knock over whoever is behind it,' he said with confidence. Shelley just nodded in a stunned 'I don't know if I can do this' kind of reply. She felt sick and unsteady in herself. The continuous sound of shuffling came to an abrupt halt the other side of the kitchen door. Kevin's hands were still shaking as he tried to keep the light fixed to the handle. Slowly the tarnished brass doorknob began to rotate, clicking with every movement.

'Get ready, Shell,' Kevin said readying himself for the impact. The door creaked open and the two children ran screaming at it. There was a massive problem when they arrived, because they didn't realise until they impacted it... it actually opened inwards and in their haste to escape, had forgotten that. The two teenagers bounced off the panel and fell backwards onto the floor. Kevin instantly lost his torch, which crashed to the ground and broke, leaving them in total darkness.

Gradually the door opened and they sat dazed, waiting for their inevitable end. There was firstly a bright yellow light and behind that a short, crouched, shadowed figure. Shelley and Kevin squinted and held their hands up to shield their eyes. The figure moved inside! Once they could focus and the intruder eased back his oil lamp, they could see that he was an old man. His head seemed electrified with bristly grey hair that tipped over onto soft blue eyes. His swollen rosy cheeks and fluffy white moustache gave him a cuddly appearance. He also had big banana fingers, which held the lamp rigidly.

'Get up, quickly,' the old man uttered in a dry, calm voice. Kevin and Shelley were really shocked and obediently got to their feet. He didn't sound threatening at all. 'He's coming just over the rise, he won't be long. You must hide,' he mumbled as he turned and made his way along the passageway. Kevin and Shelley followed tentatively after him.

'Hold on, who are you?' Kevin plucked up the courage to ask.

'Wha...' the man stopped in mid flow, 'We haven't time for this. Shadrack and his wolves are almost on the edge of town,' the man persisted with concern, 'And no doubt he'll have those Plog things in tow. If you must know, I'm Davenport. This was my home before, well, you-know-what.' He was more or less jogging on the spot, edging to move on. 'Come on, he'll be here soon.'

The words 'Shadrack' and 'wolves' were enough to jolt Shelley and Kevin into action. The old man was already making his way across the corridor and over to a darkened corner. The strong amber light from his lamp filled every crevice and left shadow in his wake. Kevin glanced at Shelley in confusion and shrugged his shoulders. The old man stopped and so did his followers. Davenport lifted his lamp and studied the wall for a moment, like an archaeologist would study a cave painting. Kevin glanced around; there was a small table to one side with a vase sitting on it and a huge painting that the old man was examining next to it.

'What's he doing?' Shelley asked Kevin in a whisper. His lips were pursed and he just shook his head in bewilderment. Davenport put the lamp on the table next to the vase and began running his right hand over the frame of the painting.

'It's here somewhere, ah, here it is,' he mumbled and reached up and pressed something on the side of the frame. With that, the painting slid away revealing a small hole behind it. Davenport picked up the oil lamp and held it in front of him. The amber glow penetrated the inside and a small windowless room befell them.

'Go on, in you go. Quickly, before he catches you,' Davenport insisted.

'What? In there?' Kevin asked nervously with an air of reluctance.

'Yes, yes, go on or you'll be caught for sure.' Davenport insisted, prodding his lamp into the hole.

'I don't know, Kev' Shelley said doubtfully.

'Couldn't we have the lamp? It's dark in there,' Kevin pointed out.

'No, no, if the light should escape, it would surely give you away,' he said, and, thinking about it, it did make sense to the teenagers.

'What about you?' Shelley asked.

'Don't worry about me, I've been hiding here for years on and off,' he said with confidence and an appreciative smile.

Kevin looked at Shelley and gave her a nod. He seemed genuine enough, he thought, and what choice did they have? They wandered reluctantly inside the blackened room and the door shut swiftly behind them! Shelley reached out and gripped Kevin's waiting hand and they stood in silence and waited.

A couple of minutes later the entrance opened and the old man peeped in.

'Here, take this.' He handed them some bread and a small container of water and closed the entrance again. The pair stood in the dark eating the bread and Shelley took a few gulps of the water.

'I don't like this, Kev.' Shelley's voice trembled in the thick overwhelming bleakness of the compartment. Kevin gripped her hand more tightly.

They waited for what seemed like forever and Kevin couldn't stand it any longer. He fumbled for the door and tried to push it open, but it was set fast.

'What are you doing, Kev?' Shelley whispered.

'I don't like this at all. Something's wrong, I can feel it.' Kevin's fear filled Shelley with dread. He pressed his ear to the wooden panel listening for some sign of hope. He closed his eyes and concentrated his mind.

'What's happening out there, Kev?' Shelley asked, breaking his train of thought.

'Shh, keep your voice down, Shell. I'm trying to listen.' Kevin was trying so hard to listen that the pressure he applied hurt his ear, so he pulled away. 'It's no good, it's just too thick to penetrate.'

'I'm scared, Kev. What if they are threatening that poor old man?' Shelley's voice trembled. 'He was only trying to help us.'

'There's nothing we can do but wait,' Kevin sympathised.

There was a click and the door began to slide open again. Hope once more filled their hearts. Cold air rushed into the small room and made Shelley and Kevin shiver. Davenport popped his head in and lit up the room with his lamp. He smiled warmly over the glow of the flame.

'Come on, it's safe now,' he said cheerfully.

Feeling relieved the two children walked past Davenport and out into the drawing room. Shelley held on tightly to Kevin's hand once more as they walked out. The brightness from Davenport's lamp bathed the room in a soft light and was complimented by another that was placed on the table. This brought more light into the room. To their utter disbelief and dismay, there in front of them stood the daunting figure of Shadrack Scarrat!

Kevin's joy turned to anger at being betrayed by their supposed new friend. He cursed himself for falling into the trap and putting Shelley in danger also. He was just about to turn and make his escape with Shelley's hand gripped firmly in his, when the familiar throaty growls of the Razzard Wolves, Ripper and Crusher, erupted behind them. Shelley thought her heart would explode and Kevin clenched his teeth in disgust. There was no escape; they were well and truly trapped!

'Hand over the brooch,' Shadrack said, his eyes fixed on them. He reached out his knobbly hand and gestured for them to place the stone in his palm.

'We-we don't have it,' Shelley surprisingly piped up.

'Don't mess with me, girlie. Give me that diamond.'

The teenagers could feel the hot breath of the wolves on their backs. Kevin knew he had no choice and reached into his pocket.

'Don't be stupid and try something silly..., b-o-y, will you?'

Shadrack's slow deliberate drawl irritated Kevin. His mind was empty of any plan to escape; his only thought was to protect Shelley. An icy cold breath of air gently caressed the nape of Kevin's neck and he shuddered, which then suddenly gave him an inspiring idea. In one swift movement he turned and saw a gap in a partly opened window. With great speed he quickly tossed the stone straight through it. Shadrack eyed his fast disappearing prize in total shock.

'NOOO!' he bellowed. Shelley also looked on in utter surprise. Shadrack was stunned and his mouth dropped open like a loose door hinge. The animal instincts of the wolves were to fetch, and they ran after the stone and burst through the wooden window... shattering it in a thunderous clatter!

This commotion gave Kevin his chance. He pulled Shelley's arm and made for the front door, while Shadrack was still reeling in shock. The old hunter burst into life again and grabbed his own lamp.

'Find that stone, boys,' he shouted through the opening. Without any other thought he immediately followed his pets and dived through the gaping hole where the window had just been. He fell onto the ground outside and dropped his lamp, which died.

The youngsters sped along the dimly lit corridor and had almost made it to the porch, when Davenport appeared and blocked their path. They hadn't seen the old man slip away when they encountered Shadrack. Now his sweet smile had vanished and in its place were a devilish scowl and a mouth full of gritted teeth.

Kevin, though, didn't stop, and Shelley, being pulled along, didn't stop either. They ran headlong into the old guy's body, knocking him to the floor and winding him badly. Davenport looked close to death, his face flushed and his mouth open, gasping for air. In a moment of exasperation the old man sucked in one huge lungful of air and lay almost ghost-like.

'We've killed him, Kev,' Shelley cried, 'We've killed him.'

'No we haven't, he's just winded,' Kevin said as he recovered quickly and pulled open the front door. He and Shelley raced off the porch and disappeared into the night.

Behind them they could hear the howls of the

wolves and the devastated tones of Shadrack Scarrat ringing in their ears. Shadrack had retrieved and relit his lamp and was groping around on all fours, searching through the grass. The wolves were sniffing and whimpering in a desperate effort not to get a beating from their master.

'Where is it? Where is that brooch?'

Shadrack's ranting could be heard some distance away, but Kevin and Shelley didn't wait to hear anymore; they sped away as fast as their legs could carry them!

'Come on, Shell, quickly, before he... realises we've escaped,' Kevin panted.

Shelley just held on and hoped that in the darkness they wouldn't run headlong into any obstacles. In her mind, all the time, was the vacant look of Davenport's eyes and the stillness of his body. Over and over in her mind was the worrying thought that they might have killed the old man!

Chapter 21

Eve

'Kevin, Kevin, I can't go any further... we-must-stop,' Shelley gasped and bent over, dropping her hands to her knees. Her lungs were striving for oxygen and her mouth widened to take it in.

'He's not that far behind us, Shell. As soon as he realises, he'll be onto us, come on!' Kevin tugged at her arm once more. Shelley took a large gulp of air and peered into Kevin's eyes.

'We've killed that man, Kevin, don't you understand? We've killed him.' She burst into a flood of tears.

'Look, Shell, you might be right, he could be dead. I don't think he is, but he could be. But if Shadrack finds us we'll also be dead,' Kevin said.

'He's not interested in us anymore anyway... he's got what he wants.' She lifted her head and sobbed. 'It's all over,' she sighed heavily. 'I don't know why we are running.'

'No... he hasn't got the...'

Shelley stopped whimpering so hard and looked up at Kevin in the new light that was daybreak. The shadows were dwindling and dawn was breathing life back into the land and she could see Kevin's facial expression.

'He hasn't... what, Kev?' Shelley asked, with a hint of confusion.

'Come on, let's go,' Kevin quickly interrupted and a

quiet smile rolled over his reddened, flushed cheeks. Shelley was intrigued.

'Kevin, he hasn't got what?' she repeated and stood her ground, half serious, half grinning; she knew after all this time travelling with Kevin that he was hiding something.

'All right, all right, he hasn't got the brooch.' He stared at her with smiling eyes. 'And to be honest, I don't think that Davenport guy is dead either, Shell. Please stop worrying, yeah?'

Shelley's eyes went wider than they'd ever gone before. She let the thought of Davenport slide for a moment and concentrated on Kevin's other comment.

'Bu-but you threw it out of the window. I saw you,' she insisted, rolling the memory round and round in her head like a film reel.

'No, actually, I threw a stone ornament out the window and he's bound to have realised that by now, so come on,' he admitted.

Shelley had regained her composure and was beaming with a new zest for life.

'You clever thing... Let's go then,' she added, and off into the dense forest they bounded, excited at keeping the brooch, but wary of being followed at every instant.

It was full daylight when they stopped and rested behind a tree trunk. The tree root was embedded inside a grassy hump which overhung a dirt road. A trickling stream lazily wound its way below them and disappeared into a culvert. Before they rested, they thirstily scooped up mouthfuls of cool water to quench their dry mouths. After taking in their fill, for a few moments they sat back and closed their eyes. The chill of morning was fast disappearing and the warmth of another day filled them with dreams. Eventually, off they drifted into a light slumber.

Shelley was the first to wake to the sound of far-off voices. She sat up half asleep and it dawned on her something was wrong! Sharack was onto them!

'Kevin, Kevin, Kevin... wake up, come on wake up, Scarrat's coming.' She gripped him and shook him vigorously.

'Wha....' he mumbled. 'What are you doing?' he said sleepily.

'Shh, they'll hear you. Shadrack Scarrat is coming.' Shelley dug him in the ribs.

'Who? Wha? Where?' He quickly came round and vigorously rubbed his eyes. Shelley was crouched to one side of the tree stump listening hard, trying to see who was coming. They didn't have time to run; they would be caught for sure.

'Not too close, they'll see you,' Kevin whispered, annoyed with himself for sleeping. The chattering was getting closer, but neither Kevin nor Shelley could make out what was being said and who was saying it.

'It can't be Scarrat, Shell. If it was, his wolves would have sniffed us out by now,' Kevin responded quietly in her ear.

'If not Scarrat, then who?' Shelley probed.

Kevin shook his head and tried to see for himself, but he too couldn't look without giving the game away. Shelley pulled at Kevin to move out of the way for her to take another look. To her complete surprise when she peeped over the jagged bark she came face to face with a beady-eyed beast. She let out a piercing screech and the beast screeched back. Terrified, she overbalanced and then, before Kevin could help her, tumbled head first down the banking and onto the road! Kevin dived down to save her, and he too rolled down the grassy slope and landed on top of her. They sat up and came face to face with Katie, Lord Fairbourne and eventually Monkey... Kevin was the first to speak.

'L-Lord Fairbourne, you-you're alive.' Kevin was absolutely stunned.

'Yes, Kevin, it would seem so.' The velvet tone of Lord Fairbourne's voice was a comforting change to that of the gravelled, throaty growl of Shadrack Scarrat. He peered at Shelley and spoke. 'Are you all right, Shelley?' He asked in a soothing tone.

'Yes, thank you.' She was puzzled and felt as though she'd met him before. Then she saw her friend. 'Katie, you're all right?' she sobbed.

'Shell, are you all right, too?' Katie cried back and they both hugged each other. Then Katie whispered into Shelley's ear, 'Where did you find him? He's gorgeous.'

'Katie we're not... you know... we're just friends,' Shelley confessed with embarrassment.

'I don't mean to interrupt a reunion, but my son isn't far away, and if he hasn't got the brooch by now he'll still be looking for it and we must keep it from him,' Lord Fairbourne disrupted the proceedings.

Shelley released herself from her hug with Katie.

'You're Shadrack's father?' Shelley gasped. 'Then

why wouldn't you give us up to him?'

Kevin looked at Shelley with an element of shock.

'Because he saved me from Shadrack Scarrat, Shell. That's how I met him,' Katie swooped in defensively.

'I-I'm sorry, Lord Fairbourne. I didn't mean to disrespect you,' Shelley apologised realising her mistake.

'That's quite all right, Shelley. You've been through a lot.' He gave a warming smile. Then Shelley suddenly remembered about the brooch.

'Kevin has the brooch,' she announced with satisfaction and Kevin nodded with confidence.

'Well done, Kevin. At least we have the power to stop him from doing anything stupid. Where is it? Show me, boy.' Lord Fairbourne extended an open hand to Kevin, who obligingly reached into his pocket and produced a shiny stone ornament!

Kevin broke into a panic and put the ornament into his left hand and dug his right hand deeper into his pocket. It wasn't there! Kevin had a frantic look on his face and glanced back at Shelley.

'But where is it, Kev? You told me you threw the ornament out through the window, not the brooch.'

'Oh dear.' Lord Fairbourne let out a low winded puff and rubbed his forehead.

'I-I must have thrown the wrong thing. In all the confusion I didn't have much time to think,' he said. Closing his eyes, he winced as if vinegar had been dripped onto an imaginary cut.

'He won't be following us, then; he will be preparing for tomorrow - the 'Dawn of Reflections,' Lord Fairbourne conveyed damningly.

'Good grief,' Monkey blurted out, and Shelley and Kevin looked on in total shock.

'That monkey spoke,' Shelley said.

'Lord Fairbourne, your monkey spoke,' Kevin remarked.

'Not you as well, Kevin... Of course, you haven't heard me talk either have you?' Monkey chuckled to himself.

'We haven't time for this banter, things are very serious. My son Shadrack Scarrat will have the power to move across worlds and also the power to destroy and I can't let that happen,' he announced with a deep worry in his eyes.

'Is there anything we can do at all?' Shelley turned to Lord Fairbourne.

'Well,' he considered as he stroked his ageing chin, 'He has the power of the stone, and he has the two most ferocious wolves at his disposal.' He shook his head, 'Don't take this the wrong way, but we are one man, three children and a monkey.'

'We're not just any children,' Kevin thundered back. 'We have got this far, so maybe we can stop him somehow.' Kevin stood resolutely as if delivering a speech before a huge battle. 'Lord Fairbourne, no disrespect, but you underestimate us.'

'Seems I have; I apologise,' Lord Fairbourne corrected.

'Lord Fairbourne, you have been through this 'Dawn of Reflections' before, to get into my world, haven't you?' Shelley asked with curiosity. 'What can we expect to happen?'

'Well, what I did was nothing really; it was all down to the brooch. At the time of the dawn breaking, the stone will shine with a brilliance that resembles the sun. That is the time when it releases a steady shaft of light which, when stepped into, takes you on the journey through to other worlds.'

'It's simple, then,' interrupted Katie. 'We must stop him getting into that light, at all costs.'

'We need a plan, a very good plan,' Kevin joined in.

'Yes, we must form a plan and force it into action at the very right time,' Monkey also stepped into the discussion. All five of them put their minds together to form a plan that hopefully would stop Shadrack Scarrat. Once they had all agreed they made their way to Settlers' Bridge.

Chapter 22

Dawn of Reflections

By the time the small group had rested and walked across country, it was starting to get dark. It was fully dark as they peered down from the mountain. They saw the flickering yellow light of a campfire that stood out in the night like a beacon. On closer inspection, they saw Shadrack and his loyal pets camped on the embankment by Settler's Bridge.

'We can't get too close or the wolves will smell our scent,' Lord Fairbourne whispered.

'I don't know about this, Kev. Now we're here it doesn't seem such a good plan after all,' Shelley said.

'Yeah, I know what you mean, Shell,' Katie interrupted, 'How are we going to get close enough to do this plan of ours?' Katie just wasn't convinced that any of it would work.

'Katie, Shelley, we must be more positive or nothing will work,' Lord Fairbourne hissed and tried to explain again. The two girls felt awkward and just listened. 'When dawn breaks, the bridge will come alive with a kaleidoscope of colour. It's then, and only then, we move in,' he said quietly. 'I don't know at this point how we are going to get close enough, because the wolves are bound to sense us coming at some point. We must not let Shadrack get to the light with the stone or everything will be for nothing, and who knows what my son is capable of.'

'Lord Fairbourne.' Kevin spoke calmly, almost losing his voice in the cold chill of the early morning air.

'What if I attract the attention of the wolves, giving you and Shelley and Katie a chance to act?'

'Err hmm,' Monkey cleared his throat indicating he was part of the team too.

'Uh, sorry, Monkey.' Kevin continued, 'And, of course Monkey. Giving you the chance of wrestling the brooch from Shadrack.' Monkey gave Kevin a look of disapproval.

'Good idea, Kevin. Well done,' Lord Fairbourne said, swelling with pride, 'that's something your father would have suggested. It's a better plan than we originally came up with.' Kevin felt warmth inside, and the memory of his father was almost too much as he held back the tears. It was still dark and so nobody could see his torment.

'I don't want to spoil your idea, Kevin, but it would be better if I distracted the wolves, because I am much more agile, and I could retreat up the nearest tree in seconds.' Kevin felt a little prang of jealousy, but then relented, realising it was a better idea.

'Well, Kevin, if Monkey can distract them we would need all the help we can get. Approaching Shadrack and his wolves will be no mean feat.' Lord Fairbourne finished by saying; 'I would feel honoured to have you at my side.'

'Thank you,' Kevin replied graciously. For the first time since being on his own in Reflections he felt as though he were a man.

The heavy blanket of black was thinning, and in its place a grained twilight. Lord Fairbourne and his followers made their way closer to the hunter's encampment. Shelley and Katie stumbled awkwardly down the loose rocky terrain. The two girls had had enough of climbing and slipping, and indeed hiding; they longed for a bath and all the girly things, like pampering, that went with it. Lord Fairbourne led the way further down and left Kevin trailing at the back, behind the girls. Monkey went on in front as scout. The air was cold and everything around them was still.

'How did you follow me, Katie, when I left the event?' Shelley asked with interest.

'Well, when we had our argument I realised how silly it was and looked out for you to make up. I saw you disappear, just before all the commotion happened, so I followed through the same door,' Katie said.

'I'd forgotten about us arguing. If we get out of this, let's make a promise never to argue again. I now realise how much real friendship means. You'll have to tell me exactly how you made it here, too. If it's anything like the journey I've had it'll be better than Niloc Snosrap's new book,' she said grinning.

'All right then, when we get out we'll both tell our stories,' Katie responded happily.

'Quiet, you two... you'll get us all caught,' Lord Fairbourne hissed back at them.

Lord Fairbourne stopped when Monkey returned.

'They're not far ahead, any further and we'll be spotted,' Monkey conveyed.

'Everyone get down,' Lord Fairbourne ordered as he crouched to the ground and peered through the thicket. Indeed they were much closer. The campfire was a brilliant blaze of yellow as sparks and smoke from the sapwood drifted high into the murky sky. The wolves were asleep, huddled together as close to the fire as they possibly could get without getting scorched. Shadrack was the other side of the fire grumbling ominously, his sinister eyes reflecting the flames.

'Monkey,' Lord Fairbourne said in dulled tones.

'Yes, master'

'It won't be long before dawn breaks. Make your way down and I'll signal when to distract the wolves.'

Monkey understood and nodded. He then silently descended the slope and moved along the grassy ground below, within a stones throw of the encampment. He steadily shuffled through the undergrowth and settled in a small rabbit hole, from where he had a clear view of the enemy camp and his friends up on the ridge.

'Good, he's in position.' Lord Fairbourne had a glimmer of excitement in his voice. 'At the very point of dawn, Shadrack has to hold the stone directly in front of the bridge.'

'He's holding it now,' Katie squeaked. 'I can see it.' She was filled with a deep excitement.

'Shhh,' Kevin hissed, 'This is not a game.'

They looked and saw Shadrack playing with something in his hands. It glinted brilliantly in the glow of the campfire. Shelley felt a burst of nervous energy through her whole body. That stone was all she and Katie needed to get home, she thought. It felt as though they could almost touch it, but there was a lot to do first, and a lot of things that could go wrong.

'We can really go home, Katie,' Shelley said, her heart thumping.

The first touch of morning appeared. Life was beginning for a new day and Lord Fairbourne was poised in readiness. They could see Shadrack, Ripper and Crusher more clearly now in the fresh light. From their viewpoint they could see the dark outline of Monkey waiting patiently. Lord Fairbourne was about to raise his hand when everything ground to a halt!

'Don't move... any of you,' an eerie voice threatened from behind.

Lord Fairbourne, Kevin, Shelley and Katie froze. Kevin slowly craned his neck and looked at Shelley and she winced. They had forgotten to mention Davenport to Lord Fairbourne; in fact, they had forgotten about Davenport completely. What a mistake to make, and now they were going to pay for it.

'He's not dead after all,' Shelley announced. She'd been beating herself up over nothing for the last day. She looked at Kevin who peered back, now wishing they had killed him.

'Shut up, turn around very slowly,' Davenport grunted.

They turned at the same time and came face to face with him and a twin barrel shotgun. He sneered and gestured with his weapon to get up. It was almost break of day and time was fast running out.

'Don't try anything stupid or I'll blast you to smithereens.' Davenport's hair was dishevelled and his expression tired and menacing. He also seemed very determined, and no one was going to test his patience at this point.

'Who are you?' Lord Fairbourne quizzed.

'That's no concern of yours, now move.' He gestured threateningly once more with his shotgun.

The three teenagers followed Lord Fairbourne down the mountain, everyone being watched by the nervous eyes of Monkey. They marched to Shadrack's camp.

'Oh my goodness, now we're in trouble.' Monkey gulped.

The luminous golden tip of the sun began to break through the surface of Reflections. Shadrack could feel the time coming and stood in anticipation. He was too embroiled in the proceedings to notice anything happening around him. His loyal wolves were awake and whimpering in the glory of a new dawn. They broke into a howling frenzy that complemented and blended with the chorus of the 'Dawn of Reflections'. The bridge stood as it had for many hundreds of years, calm and steady.

The captured party were on the scene as Shadrack reached out with the stone. A beautiful mellow crest of gold exploded over the horizon and a shimmering silver gauntlet of spangles engulfed Settlers' Bridge. A wind swooped in from nowhere and blasted its way across the land. Shadrack's face was alive with an inner peace as the exquisite diamond emitted a kaleidoscope of colour that refracted the many angles of translucent light.

The sudden shock of blinding yellow engulfed the surroundings and everyone had to shield their eyes. Davenport was also temporarily blinded and in his efforts to shield his eyes he stumbled and fell to the ground. The rifle cracked off a shot as it hit the hard ground. Kevin heard the bang even over the whooshing of the wind. Luckily for everyone concerned, the bullet propelled harmlessly and clipped the bark of a nearby tree. Kevin saw the weapon lying on the ground and in a swift movement picked it up and tossed it into the river, where it sank without a trace.

Lord Fairbourne and Katie, now realising Davenport was unarmed continued closing in on Shadrack. Shelley could see it wouldn't be long before he was transported through the time barrier. Lord Fairbourne called out for him to stop, but Shadrack couldn't hear him in the hiss of the wind and the crackling of electricity that now emitted from the core of the bridge.

'Shelley, we must stop him before it's too late!' Katie bellowed in the mangled commotion of sound. Shelley searched anxiously along the ground for something, anything, which could help them. There on the bank were stones, about the size of a couple of teacups. So she knelt down and grabbed one. The wolves, too, were preoccupied with the spectacle to notice what was going on. They were so excited they howled and howled and snarled and gnashed their teeth.

Davenport grabbed Kevin's leg and pulled the boy to the floor, while the teenager kicked frantically to release his grip. Davenport got to his feet and grabbed Kevin by the throat and began to throttle him.

Shelley lifted the stone above her head and aimed it at Shadrack. In two great movements she retracted it in the hope of getting enough propulsion to lob it at the hunter. Instead, when she quickly lifted and jerked it backwards, she lost her grip on the smooth stone and it went flying out of her hand. It whooshed backwards and caught Davenport square on the head, knocking him out cold. He slumped in surprise on top of an almost strangulated Kevin, who immediately pushed him off and gasped for air.

Without thinking about what she had just done, Shelley picked up another rock and aimed at Shadrack again. This time she tossed it in his direction and missed. It flew past and knocked the brooch out of his hand. He immediately turned in anger and stared face to face with his father. The pair locked in a deadly stare. The surge of electricity crackled and sparked in the background and the sun lifted on Settlers' Bridge and hung like molten lava with a centre that rotated into a million colours.

'It was you who helped me with the Plogs, I felt it,' he rasped. 'Now you dare to try and stop me, even after you left from here all those years ago, dear father of mine?' He spat with contempt.

'Shadrack, you can't go, I won't let you go and ruin the lives of other people on other worlds,' Lord Fair-bourne boomed back. Shadrack was already looking on the ground for the brooch, but it wasn't there!

'Where is it? I'll kill anyone who takes it,' he ranted.

Shelley was there beside them and held it in her hand, showing it to the hunter and Lord Fairbourne.

'Give it to me, girl, and I'll spare you from the wolves,' Shadrack spoke and a wry smile filled his leathery skinned face, but she held fast.

'Crusher, Ripper, come here boys.' Shadrack Scar-rat called out to his vicious pets. Even with the wind howling in their ears the wolves heard and appeared by his side. 'Now don't be silly, girlie... GIVE-ME-THE-BROOCH!' An evil filled his dead eyes, more evil that he had ever been.

'No, and if you set your dogs on me I'll throw it in the river,' Shelley said, shivering bravely. Shadrack was taken aback; his face took on a vacant look.

'No one threatens Shadrack Scarrat.' He bellowed, 'NO-ONE.'

The dogs snarled in readiness for a kill! Katie stood trembling by the side of her friend and Kevin got to his feet, but Lord Fairbourne did nothing... except utter a few simple words, which changed things forever.

'No one... except your own DAUGHTER, Shadrack.' This took everyone by surprise, most of all Shelley.

'Wha...' She couldn't utter anymore.

In total shock she dropped the diamond, and although Katie too was confused, she swiftly picked it up. No one said anything for a moment.

'I don't believe you, I haven't time for this nonsense, give me the stone,' Shadrack bellowed and reached out his hand waiting for the brooch to be returned. He caught a glimpse of Shelley's eyes and for a moment could see Allmera inside them. A part of him did not want to believe it, but also another part told him Shelley was indeed his.

Shelley looked back at her father and could also see what he had experienced.

'I-it can't be.' She too didn't want to believe it, but the feeling inside her explained a lot of things, things that had troubled her from the beginning of this journey. Why she could see the Plogs and no one else could at the World Book Day event. She now realised that she had the extra senses of her family, of her grandfather and father. How she had been abandoned in the first place, she would have to find out. It must have been her grandfather when he entered her world. He couldn't have left Reflections alone, but where was her mother?

The light on the bridge was beginning to fade, the wind dipped and the surge of power from the stone and the bridge began to fail.

'Come on, Shell, we have to go home before the light shuts down.' Katie tried to shake her friend into life again.

The wolves padded toward Shelley in a ferocious attack, but were called back by a confused and protective father in the form of Shadrack Scarrat.

'Release...release, I say, you mangy mutts.' And they obediently backed away.

'The power is draining,' Lord Fairbourne cried as the yellow sun began to fade into a burnt orange glow.

'There is only room for one person now, Katie, you must go,' Lord Fairbourne called urgently.

'No, I'm not going without Shelley,' Katie cried.

'It's all right, Katie.' Shelley gently rested her hand on Katie's shoulder, 'I'm fine. It sounds silly, but I feel I belong here. I have since the very first time I came.' Her voice was calm and soothing and Katie felt as though what she was saying she believed in.

'But Shelley, you don't belong here, you really don't. Listen to me please,' Katie sobbed.

'I don't know how, but I think she does, Katie. Now I understand how Shelley could see the Plogs. They only reveal themselves to their immediate enemy and now I know Shelley is originally from Reflections, that's how she saw them first. You came into Reflections later and invaded their world and then became an enemy to them.' Kevin spoke from Shelley's side.

'I don't understand, Shelley, I really don't. How am I going to explain to your mother and father back home?' Katie asked.

'I don't think you'll need to,' Lord Fairbourne interrupted, his face calm and his glassy eyes full of knowing.

'Wha... I don't understand,' Katie repeated.

'Quickly, there's no time, you have to go or it will be too late!'

With one almighty shove Katie was pushed through the time line. In a second she was gone and the channel closed. The 'Dawn of Reflections' sealed its own doorway and Katie was sent back home.

Chapter 23

Solo

Katie was on her knees with her eyes closed and her hands over her ears. Her face was screwed up in readiness for an impact of some kind. All felt silent and tranquil. She was curious to find out where she was, but fear willed her to keep her eyes firmly shut. A few moments passed without incident and Katie relaxed the muscles in her face, but still kept her eyes closed. Wherever she was, it was warm and calming. Slowly, to a squint at first, she opened her eyes, but it was too dark.

Gradually she lifted her tired eyelids and fully took in where she was. She turned her head from left to right and finally straight forward. It was the same dim corridor where she had previously been in the exhibition. There was the door that she had entered. Katie released her hands from her ears and dropped them to her side. It was really quiet and she tried to recollect what the exhibition was like before she had left a few days earlier. She also wondered what exhibition was going on today. She gently got to her feet and quickly felt a painful throbbing on the side of her head. Without thinking she touched her finger to the point of soreness and winced as her finger bluntly hit a large lump on her temple. I must have collided with something on the way here. She tried to think, but couldn't remember.

'Ssss, ouch,' Katie winced, sucking air between her teeth. She removed her finger instantly and ever so gently cupped the injury. It didn't feel wet, just sore, so there was no cut, but she couldn't remember how she got it. Remembering her friend, she turned around in the vain hope that Shelley had followed. There was no glittering exit, no portal, no doorway of any sort, she was on her own.

Katie turned to face the fire exit door again and walked toward it. She gripped the handle and clicked it open. The brilliant lighting of the hall hurt her eyes and she shielded them with her hand. People were filing out of the exits, the authors' tables were empty, and uniformed staff members were guiding them to the outside, just as it had been when she left. She couldn't take in all that was happening, until she looked up and saw the giant book. It all came flooding back, the huge book where Shelley must have followed the Plogs. Katie ran her eyes down from the giant book display and to the cabinet... but it wasn't there! She knew it would be empty, but there was no trace of it at all. She was confused and wandered further into the exhibition area.

'Katie, Katie, there you are, we've been worried. Come on they're all waiting by the coach to go home.' Miss Shanks wheeled up beside her in a panic and noticed the red lump on her head. 'Are you all right Katie?' she said with a deep look of concern. 'How did you do that?' she asked, and with that examined the injury.

'Oh, uh, I don't know,' Katie answered blankly.

'Good grief, girl. How did you get so dirty? Your clothes are a mess.' Miss Shanks reeled in bewilderment.

'I remember now, I fell, Miss,' Katie answered feebly.

'Come on, we'll have to take care of that back at school.' Miss Shanks gently rested her hand on Katie's shoulder to guide her toward the crowd.

'Miss.' Katie held fast.

'Yes, Katie, what is it?' Miss Shanks asked whilst still trying to move her along.

'What about Shelley?' Katie peered into the young teacher's eyes and waited.

'Shelley? Shelley who?' Miss Shanks replied with puzzlement.

'Shelley Vendor, my friend,' Katie protested.

'Ah, you found a new friend, that's good,' Miss Shanks said and smiled.

'No, Miss. Shelley from our school, she came on the trip with us, remember?' Katie retorted.

'Are you sure you're all right, Katie? Maybe we should find someone, a member of staff who can do first aid here and take care of that bump?' Miss Shanks said looking a little concerned at Katie's confused state.

'Miss, you can't remember Shelley? But she's my best friend.' Katie looked at Miss Shanks and could see that she didn't know what she was talking about. Miss Shanks then began to look around the hall. She waved to an event staff member and he approached.

'Is there something wrong?' he asked politely.

'Yes, could you find someone with first aid experience, please?' the young teacher asked.

'Certainly, what's the problem?' he asked.

'It's my pupil, she's bumped her head and she's a little confused,' Miss Shanks replied.

'Yes, of course. Follow me and I'll find someone.' The man gave a credulous look at the girl's appearance and ushered them toward him. He led the way and Miss Shanks and Katie followed with Miss Shanks holding Katie to steady her.

They were back at the entrance near the cloakroom where they had left their coats. Next to it was the first aid room. Katie hadn't noticed it before. The man knocked on the door and pushed it open. A voice called from inside, and he went in.

'Miss, I'm all right honestly, there's no need to...' But Miss Shanks interrupted immediately.

'You could be concussed; I'm having you checked out just in case.' She put on her 'I'm-in-charge face', which she didn't wear very often, especially as Mrs Gillies always took over. The man appeared again and told them to go in. Katie and Miss Shanks entered and the nurse gave her a full examination.

'How did you bump your head?' the robust nurse asked while peering at the state of her clothing. She also glanced at the teacher who could only shrug her shoulders. Katie didn't want anyone to ask her any more awkward questions, so she lied.

'I remember now. It was rushing to get an autograph before the exhibition was closed and I fell over and knocked my head on one of the platforms,' she lied convincingly.

'Ah well, there doesn't seem to be any lasting damage.' The nurse shone a small light in Katie's eyes. She also examined the fast-bruising lump which was getting darker by the minute. 'Yes, that should be fine,' she concluded, and handed a piece of paper to the teacher with the title Head Trauma printed on the top.

'If she feels dizzy or sick later tell her parents or guardian to take her to A&E,' the nurse told Miss Shanks. 'You may also get a headache later,' she added.

'I have headache tablets in my bag on the bus, Miss,' Katie recollected.

'All right,' the nurse nodded. 'When you get home, Katie, take it easy for the evening, no sports or computer games.' The nurse gave a cheery smile and looked at Miss Shanks.

'Could you make sure she gets home all right?'

Miss Shanks nodded and she and Katie made their way to the bus, and a very annoyed Mrs Gillies. Miss Shanks explained the situation to the deputy head and they got on board.

Later, after leaving the bus, Miss Shanks drove Katie the rest of the way to make sure Katie got home all right. She pulled up outside Katie's house and they walked up the path together, where her worried mother was waiting by the front door.

'Thank you for ringing, Miss Shanks,' Katie's mum uttered, 'I'll see how she's feeling in the morning.'

'Don't worry. I'd give her the day off tomorrow if I were you, just to make sure,' Miss Shanks said sensibly.

'Thank you very much, goodbye.' Mrs Hinge waved the teacher off and took her daughter inside.

'How on earth did you get this dirty, Katie, by just going to a World Book Day event?' she probed as she fussed over Katie and made her a cup of tea. This always made everyone better when they had an injury, her mother always said.

'Mum,' Katie said to her mother, still reeling after all that had happened.

'Yes, love,' her mother replied.

'Mr and Mrs Vendor across the road, have they got any children?' Katie asked curiously. Her mum looked at her with mystified eyes.

'Why no, Katie, they've lived here for years, you know they've never had any children. That bump must have really shaken you up,' she said with a worried look on her face, and added. 'They were talking once about adopting a little girl, I remember, but never did. You had better lie down for a while, Katie, just to rest your head.'

Katie did as she was told, and whilst her mother busied herself in the kitchen, Katie felt in her pocket. There was something there! It was cold and lumpy, and when she retrieved it she recognised the glinting diamond brooch from the book. She closed her eyes and rolled it around playfully in the palm of her hand.

'Shelley, I will miss you, I will really miss you,' she sobbed, as a stream of tears escaped her eyes and pooled onto the fabric of the cushion. 'I will see you again, Shell, just you wait and see.' Her eyelids became heavy and she drifted off into a deep, dream-filled sleep.

Chapter 24

A New Life

The doorway was now closed in Reflections, and Shelley stood by Kevin and Monkey, still trying to make sense of everything that had happened. Monkey's face was long and sad; he would really miss Katie. She'd only just gone and already he felt so lonely. Lord Fairbourne Scarrat and his son Shadrack Scarrat were stood by the bridge, with Shadrack's two wolves standing loyally by his side. A very sore Davenport was sitting on the ground nursing his injured head, and as totally confused as anyone. Settlers' Bridge looked no different than it did before, it stood strong and proud. The sun settled to its rich golden colour and brought back the warmth of a summer's day.

Shelley looked at Kevin and gave him a friendly smile, as if to say thank you for all your help. He didn't say anything back to her, only smiled.

'I will really miss her.' Monkey broke the silence. Shelley gave him a look of sadness.

'I will too, Monkey.'

Lord Fairbourne peered into his son's eyes.

'What do you intend to do now son?' he said, and rested his hand on Shadrack's shoulder.

'I don't know. I have a daughter now to look after.' His refrain had changed from an angry old hunter to a new kind of person, a concerned dad, perhaps it was his own father's influence. The lines on his face seemed to shallow from the gruff-looking person he usually was.

Kevin walked over to Shelley and they sat on a patch of grass beside the bridge. Shelley took a deep breath and paused.

'I have a dad and mum now, real parents. But I'll truly miss mum and dad Vendor,' she sighed.

'Shelley, this is going to be hard to take in, but once Katie stepped over the time line things changed back home for you,' Lord Fairbourne said with a hint of sadness in his voice.

'What do you mean?' Shelley pushed for an answer.

'The parents that you knew went back to not having a child, so the adoption never took place.'

'But that's...'

'Impossible?' Lord Fairbourne cut in. 'This is Reflections after all, Shelley, and you know that things happen differently here.' He pursed his lips and widened his eyes.

'Wow, that's a lot to take in after having such a crazy adventure,' Kevin piped up, and picked up a stone that was nestled in the depth of the grass and toyed with it. 'We can still be friends, though, eh?'

'What do you mean, Kev? Of course we can still be friends. Why would anything change?' Shelley looked a little mystified.

'Well, your grandfather is Lord Fairbourne Scarrat. Your father is next in line for the Lordship, and that will make you a Lady, I guess,' he said with a smirk.

Shelley gave him a playful dig in his arm with her fist and giggled.

'Friends till the end.'

'Why didn't you tell me I had a child? Father,' Shadrack probed.

'Things were getting out of hand here, son. I felt the power of the stone inside me, and it was too much to bear, so I had to go and put it somewhere out of harm's way. I had known about Allmera being pregnant a long time ago, at the time she left you. You know we were close, and I didn't want to leave Reflections without seeing her, and my newborn granddaughter. She was very frightened for the baby because you were... you were...'

'Changing, father. That's what was happening to me, I was turning evil, I know' Shadrack swiftly replied.

'Yes, all right, you were turning against everything I'd taught you.' He gave a sorrowful look at his son, 'And I was frightened for Alexa.'

'Alexa? That's her name?' Shadrack asked awkwardly.

'Yes, well the world I took her to gave her a new name and a new identity,' Lord Fairbourne admitted. 'Allmera wanted me to take her before she...'

'Before what, father?' the old hunter asked.

'Before she died. She'd had an illness after having Alexa, and a little while after giving me my grand-daughter, she passed away.' Lord Fairbourne lowered his head and closed his eyes. After a moment he raised his head once more, and opened his eyes. 'You are going to have to tell her soon, but not now, not today.'

Then a strange and wonderful thing happened. There was movement from beyond the trees. Figures began to descend from the hills and forest; one or two at first, and then lots more. They were the population of Reflections, hidden away in the mountains for years. Each and every one of them had been in hiding, waiting for the day when the Plogs would be defeated and Lord Scarrat ruled once again. Lord Scarrat smiled and waved to them, and they all gave a huge welcome cheer. They didn't have to be fearful anymore. The Plogs were gone and they didn't have to hide, they could return to their homes.

Shadrack walked over to Shelley and reached out and touched her hand, and she tentatively touched his. Monkey came up beside her and slipped his hand in hers, as they all made the long way back to Scarrat Town.

Lord Fairbourne Scarrat took over his rightful place. He lived out his days ruling Reflections until he died a very old and happy grandfather.

A reformed Shadrack Scarrat looked after his new-found daughter, and explained to her how he had met Allmera and how they'd argued and she'd run away, never to return. He was a different man then, and had treated her badly; he now regretted it with all his heart.

Lord Fairbourne, before he died, had also explained to Shelley about how he had blessed Allmera's wishes by taking Alexa to the new world. Lord Fairbourne went on to explain that with his son in such a wild state of mind, he couldn't leave her with him; so he'd crossed the time line and started a new life in a new place. He left Alexa in an office foyer for a cleaner to find her, but didn't give her name. He didn't want her to be found out and, by disappearing himself, it would give her more of a chance to blend in with her new world. Lord Fairbourne went on to write the book and place the precious brooch on the cover. He knew such a precious jewel would be kept under lock and key and away from evil. He melted away into the background as a teacher and kept an eye on his granddaughter, Shelley, as she grew up; and also on the stone. He never guessed that the Plogs would one day find his path and seek the stone for Shadrack.

It took a long while for Shelley to settle into her new role and she was sad for quite a while. But with Kevin and Monkey's help, and the new-found love of her father and grandfather, she eventually felt part of her natural world. She often thought of her adopted parents and Katie; those memories were stored in the back of her mind. Reflections, though was her home, now and forever...

Meet The Author

Colin R. Parsons lives in the Rhondda Valley, South Wales, in the UK. He is married to Janice and they have two sons, Kristoffer and Ryan.

He loves to write fantasy, and the surrounding mountains, lakes and forest feature in his work. He has already written the *Wizards' Kingdom* series, a thrilling three-part adventure. He also loves reading, and when he has any free time, can be found with a good fiction book.

His ambition is to write lots of books for all ages to read and enjoy.

—

**The next book in the series is
The Curious World of Katie Hinge**